SHIFTING SANDS

An Island Romance

Karen Dodd

Published by Karen E. Dodd Publishing Company
6304 Albatross Dr.
New Bern, NC 28560
www.geocities.com/kedodd2/index.html

(252) 514-2953
Other books in print by this author include:

Carolina Comfort ISBN 0-9707197-4-4
Carolina Comfort II ISBN 0-9707197-2-2
Down East on Nelson Island ISBN 978-0-9707197-3-7
Begin Again, Quinn ISBN 978-0-9707197-5-1

Cover art by Carl Hultman.
http://www.artfactorynewbern.com/index.php?id=10&detid=59
Call 252-633-1845 for more information. Another place to find his work is
http://www.creativeshake.com/profile.html?MyUrl=hultmansart
Thank you, Carl for painting Island Home for my *Shifting Sands*.

***

Although the book takes place near Southport, NC, there is no Harrold's Island near the mouth of the Cape Fear River. All names and/or actions in the story are figments of the writer's imagination.

Acknowledgements

Where would I be without writing friends to analyze, cajole and share the burden of all this creativity? Thank you to the Low Country Charleston 2007 group, Java Writers of New Bern, Harbour Book Club, Hearts of Carolina Romance Writers' critique groups for their suggestions and Rosie Wood and Christine Grotheer for their editing expertise.

DevinCage@poachersportsfishing.com *confirmed my fishing information. Trips to Bald Head Island and Shackleford Banks inspired the setting. Southport, with its waterfront, shops, restaurants, houses, antique stores and galleries, proves to be a great location, not only for movie making, but also storytelling. The smell of salt air kept me focused. Carl Hultman let me wander around his studio and ask a few painter questions. Dr. Bill Ramseur, retired oncologist, assisted me with the cancer, treatment and side effects information. Hubby, Denton, read this several times and encouraged me to keep going.*

Thank you all.

ONE

Anne Basnight threw her Blackberry against the wall, but the annoying musical notes of "Dixie" continued.

Mother, you never call me and today you've tried a half dozen times. Why?

Frustrated, Anne stomped across the room, picked up the humming handheld, stuffed it under a pile of cushions on her window seat and sat on it. As she pondered her predicament, she watched black hooded laughing gulls screech at each other on the dock pilings outside. The Oak Island light winked across the inlet and even the sea oats seemed to be waving, mocking her attempt at escape.

Anne had driven to Uncle Eddie's house to hide her Mini-Cooper in his garage, knowing relatives would not visit there until summer.

No one's going to notice this thirty-something woman strolling barefoot down the street, an attaché case in hand.

She'd pulled off her Manolos and walked several blocks to her own family's home beneath moss draped oak trees, removed the key from under the dead geranium's pot and let herself inside. *I haven't taken a vacation since Daddy died. Ten and a half years was a long time to wait for a holiday.* She brooded over her decision to leave her responsibilities behind and begin doing the things she wanted in life. *I want a family of my own.*

Beneath her butt, the phone chirped again. The different tone told her it was the office calling this time.

Millie, I left you a note not to bother me. What can be so important that it won't wait three more days? It's a weekend doggone it! I need this time away to follow through on some major decisions.

She walked across the Aubussan carpet and opened a drawer in the armoire. A flick of her fingers allowed her skirt to drop to the floor followed by the jacket and blouse. Kicking them to a corner of the room, she pulled on a pair of cut-off jeans, positive that she wore the same size she had as a teenager. Anne tugged a neatly folded camp tee shirt from the drawer and slid it over her head.

Pausing a moment, she stroked the dark pearl fastened to her navel ring, a reminder of her rebellious years. She'd had her navel pierced to shock her father, but he never noticed. The pearl under her tailored suits and party dresses had become her private talisman for independence.

When the phone chirped once more, she left the bedroom. Anne pulled the crocheted throw from the couch and wrapped the warmth and comfort of the green and blue yarns around her as she glided open the glass door. Her parent's generation of Basnights had enclosed the screen porch to make the Carolina room. When she cracked the vertical swing-out windows, the sea breeze blew in, cooling her body.

Concentrate and focus here, Anne, not back there. Oh, God, am I depressed or what? Anne tried to empty her mind, but years of multi-tasking refused to temper her thoughts. For the fourth month in a row, her monthly flow had promptly started and stopped, like clockwork. *It has to be the fertility medicine they put me on. I want this baby so much! Why can't my body give me something that every other woman since the beginning of time has been able to do?*

Her body refused to nurture the donated sperm. Pressing her flat stomach beneath the denim shorts, she imagined it swollen with a baby.

Foregoing the normal route of marriage and a husband, because she didn't have the time to find a suitable mate, she decided six months ago to use an invitro fertilization procedure at the Charlotte clinic. Her biological clock was ticking away the months and she still wasn't pregnant.

Her briefcase held the answer. Inside the leather attaché were tucked her new fertility drugs and a large tan envelope. Tonight she would pull out all of the contents, spread the documents on the breakfast room table and plot a future with no business pressures, her mother's dependence or that nagging memory of her brother's death.

Stop thinking about it all. Lose the stress, Anne. That will help you conceive.

She ached to be free from the constraints of management and employees doting on her. She barely had time for her morning workout and a chat with her mother before leaving for the office. The workday was never long enough to finish the required papers and attend the necessary meetings.

A tight stomach, migraine headache and an occasional paper cut were her evening rewards from the day. Anne's stomach churned. She tolerated the dizziness too. The doctor warned her that an abrupt stop to the medications would increase the symptoms. She checked her watch to be certain she didn't miss her next dose.

Anne patted her tummy.

When you're born, Mommy will read you stories every night and bring you to the beach. I plan to live here or maybe on the island across the inlet. No child of mine will be left to make up imaginary friends or to pester others.

The Blackberry warbled once more distracting her thoughts.

For God's sake, Millie, why are you calling me on a Friday afternoon? Read the post-it note I stuck on your computer screen. I explained everything. I am not going to answer any calls while I'm on vacation.

***

After dark, she munched on peanut butter and jam cracker sandwiches as she studied the documents from her briefcase. It was midnight when she closed the case, planted it in the back of her closet and shut the door. *Where else does one hide a million dollars worth of dreams?* She grinned satisfied that her plan was justified.

***

The next morning, Anne dropped the annoying Blackberry into the dishwasher with her empty teacup, shut the door and started the wash cycle.

Why didn't I think of this before? Mischief beamed from her face for the first time in a dozen years.

A warm spring wind blew across the back of the house. Removing her watch and rings, she dropped them into the empty sugar canister by the kitchen sink. She pulled back her hair into a blunt pony tail. An old halter-top, a faded bathing suit bottom and pair of dirty tennis shoes suited her planned day. When she was a child, Anne escaped from her father by taking out her sailboat. Carefree at last, she grabbed a canvas bag of supplies and headed for the dock. Relief worked its way up from her toes, past her pierced navel and smoothed the creases on her forehead.

The engine started easily and she steered the small boat into the waterway. Her body tingled in anticipation. The inlet between her home and the ocean spanned four miles. When she crossed the mouth of the Cape Fear River, Anne pointed the boat into the wind and cut the engine. The sail flapped as she tugged it up and secured the line. The teak had grayed under the sun over the years, but the craft responded to her touch. Finally confident in herself and the old boat, she wrapped a piece of cloth around herself, like a pareo, to minimize the sunburn on her back and legs.

She hadn't thought about work for hours and it felt good. When she remembered the attaché hidden in her closet, she grinned about that stroke of luck. In her mind, she balanced the investments she would make, like a child playing with wooden blocks.

Daddy, you schooled me well in the business, but I'm determined not to let your bitter memory intrude. When you weren't entertaining business associates, you were with your courtesan-of-the-week, driving Mother further into her cocktail hours. How many affairs did she endure?

Mama, you were like a moth fluttering around Daddy when he did come home. Didn't you realize how annoying you were? I was embarrassed for you. And Teddy, you were a selfish brother using your charm to persuade us to do whatever you wanted. I hated you for that.

Anne threw crusts from her sandwich into the water, counting off her dysfunctional family members. She watched the crumbs drift behind the boat until a seagull floated down, settled in the water and dined on her discarded lunch.

Her mind snapped back to the present when a gust of wind batted the sail. The sun was still shining but the air puckered with instability. Thunder rolled across the ocean as she turned the boat back to shore. Clouds, like black knuckles, pounded the horizon with bolts of lightning.

She felt a jolt and peered over the stern. Only one rusted pin held the rudder to the transom. Several waves later, that pin sheared and her rudder floated away. Her concern increased as she tried to grab the rudder with a boathook. The wind snapped the sheets from her hand. Anne struggled to regain them, but the loose lines burned welts across her face and arms.

Shoving her arms into her life vest, she felt the boat shudder under another blast. There was little time to think as fear chilled her body. Working her way forward to the mast, she unfastened the halyard and lowered the sail, fighting it onto the boom. The weight of the rain flattened the waves, as well as her hair against her head. An angry fist of clouds opened like a palm smacking her boat.

As the rain increased, the cold stinging drops thumped her body into action. The engine would do little good without a way to steer the boat. Overhead the halyard snapped against the mast in a never-ending rattle. Resolute, she stood to look for the flare gun.

This storm will not be the end of me.

For a split second, she wished she were in her office this Saturday reviewing the never-ending paperwork. The boom swung, smacking her head. Her fingers grabbed the empty air.

Ouch! I'm falling overboard. This can't be happening! I'm Anne Basnight, CEO and caretaker of the family legacy. What will they do without me?

TWO

The smell of bacon pulled Anne from a deep sleep. She rolled over and stretched, brushing the sleep from her eyes, then jerked back when an Irish setter sat up beside her. Tail slapping on the floor, the dog yawned and breathed doggy breath into her face. He shoved his head under her hand, pleading for a pat. Faded drawstring curtains flapped in the breeze, drawing her gaze past the louvered doors to a deck. Her foggy mind recognized the sound of ocean waves crashing and the cries of laughing gulls somewhere near. She gasped, seized by dread. *I don't eat bacon, live by the ocean, own a dog or sleep naked!*

Pulling herself up from the rumpled king-sized bed, she scanned the room, looking for her clothes and purse. Years of self-taught restraint controlled her panic. Her confidence only needed a bit of shoring up and everything would be fine. She wrapped a soft quilt around her body and stood up. The room swirled around her so she put a hand on the bedpost to steady herself. Dizziness receding, she gingerly made her way across the creaking floor to the adjoining bathroom. *No clothes here either! Where am I?*

Who am I?

She turned back into the bedroom and searched the massive wardrobe. A row of blue jeans and a few collared shirts hung in precise order. Tee shirts lay folded in a bottom drawer. She grabbed a pair of faded jeans and held them up to her waist. *Hmm, they seem to fit. These look familiar.* Her hands trembled as she pulled them on.

The length was right for her height, but when she tugged them on, the waist dropped low on her hips. Shrugging into a floral print shirt, fingers fumbling with the shirt's top buttons, she gave up and tied a knot with the bottom corners of the shirt tail.

Still woozy, she walked through the French doors and peered over the dunes. *Nothing familiar. Why can't I remember? Do I live here?* Holding the porch railing, she stood on tiptoes to glimpse the flat waters of the sound and a distant shoreline. She had no memory of anything prior to seeing the red dog that now sat on his haunches watching her every move. *He seems to know me. Are you my dog, fellar? This doesn't feel right, but how do I know that?*

The clatter of dishes and pans drew her to the top of the stairs. Her attention focused on the back of a man working over a stove. He wore a plaid shirt tucked into ragged jeans. His bare feet scuffed the worn linoleum floor as he moved about. The dog nudged past, leading her down the steps.

"Oh!" Her startled cry caused the man to turn.

"Sorry. I know I'm not a pretty sight. I didn't think you'd be up so early." He set his breakfast plate on the table and grabbed a Carolina ball cap cupping it over the angry scar that crossed his bald head. “Good morning.” He faced her again. “How are you feeling?”

Her stomach jerked as she swayed against the stair railing. She balled her fists and demanded, “Who are you? Are you some kind of pervert?”

“No, calm down. *You* invaded *my* space yesterday. I’d like nothing better than to send you back where you came from.” He tucked his hands in his pockets studying her. “Do you remember how you got here?”

“I don’t even remember my name.” Frustrated, she studied the kitchen’s varnished pine walls, open cabinet shelves and pantry. An arched doorway opened to the living room. The staircase divided the two lower rooms. Looking out the kitchen window over the sink, she saw sand dunes and outbuildings. “What did you do with my clothes?” His cheek bones shifted back and forth, as he swished his coffee. He stared back with a blank face.

Under his gaze, she stood tall, running her fingers through her shoulder-length auburn hair. “You don’t remember?” He didn’t believe it, but he thought he’d play along. Her face had changed in the twenty years since he last saw her.

“No. Do you know who I am?”

She had grown up, but still had that determined chin-poked-out stance she had when she wanted something as a child. Her posture indicated she was used to giving orders. Her hundred-dollar haircut shouted class. "Nope, I haven't a clue," he lied, continuing her charade. "I'd like to know how you got here."

He pointed up the steps. "You tell tales when you dream. They sound more like nightmares -- as if you're running away from someone. Do you know who that might be?" He watched a frown plow two vertical creases between her eyebrows. "This is my home. I'm here because I chose to be here, alone. I like solitude while I paint."

One of her eyebrows rose at that information.

"Pictures, to sell. I don't bother anyone, but you washed up yesterday morning, looking like a drowned rat and intruding on my time."

When her frown deepened, he relented. "You're looking better now, maybe a little puffy around the eyes."

Her hands flew to her face. "Doesn't hurt much, no stars or blurred vision, if you're interested."

He nodded at her with his chin. "I didn't know if my clothes would fit, but you're a tall one. We'll have to get you something to keep those pants up." The tied knot just beneath her breasts exposed a narrow ribbon of skin. The pants hung below her pierced navel, revealing a flat stomach. She gave them a tug. He added, "Where did you find my Hawaiian shirt?"

"Upstairs, in the wardrobe," she whispered as she edged her way around the kitchen. Her hands trembled as she touched the countertop. "Do you have a newspaper, television, something to help me remember?"

He watched as her gaze moved slowly from him around the kitchen. “Relax, I bet you’ll remember it all before the day is out. You have a bump on your head. Does it hurt?” He didn’t believe for a minute she’d lost her memory.

“I’m fine, not to worry. I need to leave.” Her hand felt the knot on her forehead, “Ouch,” while her stare settled on the wall-mounted knife rack.

“Calm down, I said you’re safe here. You need to relax. You’ll remember.” He selected the narrow boning knife and stepped towards her.

She backed away shaking her head. “No! Please…”

“Stop that, now.” He flipped the knife, holding the blade and offered the ebony handle. “Here, feel safer?”

Gripping the knife, she stood her ground. “I don’t understand. I can’t remember my name, what kind of car I drive or anything about you.” She squinted as if trying to recall. “Was I drugged? Is that how you got me here?”

“No drugs.” He stepped back to his side of the table and picked up his coffee mug. “Believe me when I say you arrived here on your own.”

“Hungry?” He ignored her pointing knife as she shook her head. He pulled out his chair. “I need to eat my breakfast. It’s getting cold.” He sat down at the round pedestal table and began sopping his egg with a piece of toast. As he bit into a crisp bacon strip, he wondered what he was going to do with her.

“No. I’m not hungry.” She wrinkled her nose as she explained. “The smell of bacon makes me sick.”

"Sorry I didn't know about the bacon." He shifted in his chair remembering her childhood belligerence. She wouldn't go away while he worked. He chuckled. "It would be hard for you to go home if you can't remember where that is." He knew her home was over 300 miles away. The family's coastal home in town, if they still owned it, was across the sound. "You're on an island." *Why had she come back and landed on his island? How could she end up on his beach without a memory?*

"I told you! I don't know where I'm from."

"Alright, so you say." He walked to the sink, rinsed out his mug, reached into a side cupboard and grabbed a new cup. He took an aluminum percolator from the range top and poured. "Coffee?"

"No thank you, I don't drink coffee. Do you have any tea?"

"You like tea? This isn't a restaurant, but…." He bent, looking in the lower cabinet for a box of tea. "How do you know you don't drink coffee?"

Her frown deepened the ridge across her sunburned forehead, but she slowly shook her head again.

"When I first moved to this island I could barely walk over one sand dune." He didn't look back as he searched. He was growing tired of her game. He stood up with a box of tea. "I eat, then I walk and after that, I paint every morning. I have a routine, see?"

She nodded. She had the grace to blush, which frustrated him.

"I'm selfish about my island, my time and my tea!" He dropped the box of packaged tea on the table, which startled her. "I carry a mug of coffee when I walk. We find things thrown up on shore, but never found a woman before. You drank my coffee. You were shaking with cold. I could hardly get you back here and up the stairs." He realized he had shuffled back into his father's brogue with burred words. Some vowels he swallowed while others lingered in his mouth. Words with one syllable words like 'I' and 'here' became two. "Casey saw you first."

The dog looked up at the sound of his name.

"You drank a lot of coffee. I had to warm you up once I got you here."

"*That's* the reason my mouth tastes like salt and stale coffee," she exclaimed. "In fact it's turns my stomach just thinking about it. *Uh-oh*!" She spun around, dropping the knife and ran back up the stairs to the bathroom.

He heard her vomiting and followed her up the steps. "Are you alright?" He grabbed a clean washcloth and turned on the water spigot. Wringing it out, he handed it over. "Yep, you did a lot of throwing up. You probably swallowed too much salt water." He hesitated before asking, "You're not pregnant are you?"

"Oh, God!" She straightened herself up and then sat on the toilet seat clutching the cool terrycloth to her face. "I don't know if I'm married much less, pregnant. Does this look like a wedding band?" She held up her hand showing him a faint band of un-tanned skin on her ring finger. She looked up at him and shock replaced the misery in her eyes. "You don't have any eyebrows."

"Chemotherapy. It's been over six months, now. They say it worked." He squatted on the floor next to her and looked up from under his hat brim. "I lost all my hair. I have no idea when it will come back, if it does." He stood up. "Feel better now?" She stood wavering and turned once more to dry heave while he held her. He tapped the bottom of the commode with his bare toe, empathizing with her. "This past year, that toilet and I have done a fair amount of hugging."

Her mouth dropped open. "Oh, I'm sorry." She snapped it shut. Her face bloomed gradually, as her lips filled with color. The even fullness of both her lips fascinated him. The green eyes used to hex him with curses when she didn't get her way.

What am I thinking? Lips, eyes, skin! He offered his hand to help her stand upright. "Come on. Let's see if I can fix your tea. Do you feel like eating a piece of dry toast, maybe?" He led her out of the bathroom and back down the stairs. If she was telling the truth, he felt a tad protective. He'd give her a couple of days to remember before he turned her over to the police. He wouldn't want them to find her without a memory.

THREE

Anne hesitated after following him to the kitchen. She leaned against the counter where she restored the knife to its proper place. “No, I don’t think I can eat. Who are you? You haven’t told me your name.” The barrier between them had shifted now that he had held her as she threw up in his bathroom, an intimacy she didn’t care to repeat. She was more curious than scared.

He looked out over his sandy backyard. “Well, it doesn’t seem fair that you don’t know your name when I know mine. Why don’t we make up names for each other? Would that make you more comfortable? What kind of name should I have?” He smirked pointing to his head. “Now, don’t say Jean-Luc or Lex Luthor.”

She slanted her head studying his face. He did look a bit like Captain Picard of the USS Enterprise, but maybe more like Daniel Craig, the latest James Bond. His shirt fit snugly across his chest. His faded jeans hugged his hips like a glove. *How can I remember an actor’s name and not my own?*

She smiled at her host. Only the hat seemed out of place, covering his bald head and hiding the ugly scars. “I’ll play your game. Do you live here by yourself?”

He nodded. “No other homes here. This is my island and you washed up on it.”

This new situation appealed to her. He wasn’t so bad either. Perhaps, he used his gruffness to distance himself. She wasn’t afraid of him; in fact, she was intrigued with his naming challenge. She stepped closer and stood nose to nose, her bare feet almost touching his. His knees peeked out of a tear in the jeans at hers. She noted his thin nose, narrow face, deep sunken gray eyes and smooth skin. At least there were eyelashes. She smelled his muskiness and coffee breath. If she were going to be a part of the man’s island, she’d make the best of it. “I’ll call you Grayson,” she said. “Like Lord Graystoke, you know, Tarzan.”

“*Ah*, another fictional character.” Grayson tucked his hands behind in his pockets. He inhaled the space between them. For a second she imagined how his body might feel beneath his clothes. She blinked her mind elsewhere. “You have deep gray eyes and you are king of this -- island, aren’t you?”

His hat brim touched her forehead. “Yes, I am that.” His lips pressed together in a straight line. “So, shall I follow your lead and call you some derivative of Jane?” He slowly moved his hand up towards her head. He hesitated a moment then touched her hair.

She shivered.

"How about Red or Scarlet? No. One redhead already and he's as jealous as any woman."

On cue, the dog barked at them and danced back and forth. Grayson stepped back. "See? He knows I'm talking about him. I'll call you ..."

She cringed under his gaze and waited. Goose bumps ran down her spine when he pushed the lock of hair behind her ear. *Give me a nice name, please. What was it they called me in the dream? That old man was trying to grab me but I escaped.* She blinked back to pay attention.

His tongue licked his lip when he said, "Lise. How do you like that?" He pronounced the name in one syllable with a French accent. "It's your smile."

"Is that a Mona Lisa joke?" Lise, it rhymed with tease. She wrapped her tongue around the sound, repeating it to herself. "Lise," the name rolled off her tongue and through her teeth. "I like it. I feel better having a name." She looked around the kitchen, accepting its homey comfort. Relieved, as if she had escaped here from something she couldn't remember. "My name is Lise. Nice crib you've got here, Grayson." His eyes seemed to dance when she spoke his name.

She peeked into his small living room. "Did you remodel this space?"

"My grandparents lived here years ago." He poured hot water into her teacup. "Yep, before I lived here. In the summer, it gets hot; don't have electricity for air conditioning. I replaced that wall with a row of windows and screens to catch the prevailing breezes and added storage bins. I don't need a lot of space to paint and sleep. The changes suit me."

She walked over to his easel and studied the canvas. "You paint with oils?" A pleasant memory hid just out of her grasp. "I love the smell of oils."

"*Mmm*, do you now?" He took a short breath as if to sample the air with his nose. "I don't smell it anymore. I use what I learned with, not the new odorless stuff." He pointed to cans of turpentine and linseed oil. "For a while, I couldn't stand those odors of painting. That's another side effect of the chemotherapy." He turned his back on her, angry that he shared another part of himself.

He remembered her barging into his studio when she was a child, demanding he paint a picture for her school assignment. He'd gently mocked her and told her to paint her own homework. She'd pestered him until he set up another easel and coached her. They spent a week painting every afternoon until her father told him that his daughter didn't need private lessons from the baitmaster's son. His studio at the time was in the back of the family business, a bait and fishing supply store. *The old bastard never recognized that my talent made me a well-respected artist.*

He nudged his mind back to the present. "But I was going to fix you breakfast, wasn't I?" He grunted when she followed him. "Sit down here. The dog minds better than you." He held a chair and was surprised when she sat like a princess at a royal banquet.

On cue, the red dog came over to lean against her leg. Grayson watched her hands fondle the dog's ears, disturbed to experience his body yearning for her touch.

"You need something in your stomach." Grayson placed thick slices of bread on a blackened cookie sheet and slid them under the broiler. Crouching down, he watched the flames lick over the pan.

"I suppose I should thank you for rescuing me," Lise folded her hands on the table. "You have me at a disadvantage, sir." She blushed deeply this time. "You've seen me in the buff. Did I have clothes when you found me?"

"I've seen a lot of naked women in my line of work. It doesn't bother me. Don't let it bother you."

"Oh, I see, very well then." Her blush faded.

"You were wearing rags. There was a piece of cloth tied around you and a torn swim suit bottom. I threw them out. No pockets, no purse. Sorry." He pulled the tray out with a towel, flipped the bread, and slid the pan back into the broiler. "It stormed late the previous afternoon." He sucked on a scorched finger. "Do you remember that? Were you in a boat or towed from the beach by a riptide?"

Her head swung back and forth slowly. "I don't remember." She stopped to explain. "When I move my head too fast, the room spins." She leaned her head back on the tall ladder-back chair as her fingers tapped on the table top. She fidgeted in the chair drawing one leg up under her hips. "Do you have a phone?"

He looked from his toasting back at her. "Who you going to call?" He tapped his temple. "You got a number in your head?"

She reached to her waist. "If I had my cell phone, I could call one of the numbers in it, couldn't I? I wonder where I put it. Something tells me I couldn't live without it." She felt for her Blackberry. "Like it should be strapped to my body." Empty handed she placed her palms back on the tabletop.

"Wouldn't help you if you did," he replied. "You probably wouldn't have any reception out here. I don't have a telephone. I'm lucky to have electricity. I use a propane generator when I need it. The Coast Guard pulled telephone lines over when they had a station here, back in the forties. That's gone now, washed into the ocean. I come and go by boat, but mostly I stay here. Right now, the motor's not working. I could have fixed it, but you took up a lot of my time yesterday."

Her eyebrows went up, forming arches over the yellow-tinged green irises. "What about that radio?" She pointed to the vintage aquamarine radio on the top of his refrigerator.

"That was my grandparent's." He hesitated. "I never had the heart to throw it out. At night, I can pick up stations in the Midwest. It doesn't get good reception locally."

"A person can't disappear and no one looks for them. Have you heard anything about me being missing?"

He shook his head, betraying her trust once more. "Would they be friend or foe?" His fingers drummed on the back of his chair urging her to remember on her own. Apparently, the press had already convicted her without the benefit of a trial. That's why he decided to keep her on the island - just a couple of days, until she could remember.

The smell of burning toast drew their eyes back to the broiler pan.

"Damn!" He pulled the pan out with the towel and dropped it on the counter. "Here, now." He scraped the burnt edges from the crust and cut it. "Eat this slowly."

She looked at the plate. "Someone used to cut my toast into triangles like that. It makes me feel -- happy." Smiling, she picked up the toast and nibbled a corner.

"So now we know your mama cut your toast in triangles, you're used to the smell of oil paints, you carry a cell phone and you prefer tea to coffee. See. It's all coming back." He hoped she remembered in the next three days. She sipped her tea and nibbled at the bread. He turned his back and washed the dishes, piling them on the enamel drain board. "Feel like you could eat an orange?"

He grabbed a navel orange from the fruit bowl and peeled it for her, pulling the white webbing off and setting the peel aside. The sharp orange tang overpowered the burnt-toast smell. He slid the orange slice-laden plate towards her, taking a section for himself.

"Thank you." She obediently picked up one piece and looked into his eyes. "I don't think I've met you before. I also don't think you're a pervert. Sorry about that." She patted the dog. "Perverts don't have good dogs like this one." Her voice softened. "I mean I'm trying to picture you with hair and without the," she twirled her fingers around the top of her head, "you know, cancer thing." She tapped her head. "I am familiar with the way you talk. I've heard it before." She shrugged her shoulders as she picked up another section of orange and sucked on it.

Her lips and tongue worked on the orange slice. The section of orange disappeared into her mouth. Surely, she didn't realize how sensual her nibbling could be.

Lise yawned like a cat, her arms and hands stretching out across his table. "Excuse me." Her hands massaged her arms and legs. "I feel like I've run a marathon and it caught up with me."

Grayson froze when her hand reached for the last piece of orange. She sucked on this section as well. It was maddening to watch her lips work over the orange section. "We all want to run away from something." He tapped the plate of toast with a finger. "You eat like a mouse. Hurry up and finish what you want there."

He stood up. The golden boy's kid sister had grown into a beautiful sexy woman. Grayson had found her at another vulnerable time in her life and he wanted to keep her safe even though her family had shamed his. If she had lost her memory, was it his job to help her find it? Yet, he half-hoped she'd remember him.

"I need some fresh air." He thumbed toward the door. "Casey and I are going for our walk. It started as physical therapy but I discovered it helps me paint. Make yourself at home." He still wasn't convinced about the amnesia. *It all seems too convenient.*

The dog lunged toward the door as Grayson switched his ball cap for a large-brimmed floppy hat from the multi-hat rack on the wall. "Take a shower and relax. We'll be back in an hour. I have an art show and a business trip next month. I have deadlines to meet and need to get back to my painting so I'll be ready. " He snapped, "You're an interruption I don't need." The screen door slammed behind him.

He turned and stepped back. "Sorry, that didn't come out right. I'll work around you." Maybe he'd give her a week to remember it all. That seemed about right.

Before Grayson headed over the dunes, he stopped at a shed and tucked his own cell phone in a pocket. When he reached the sound side of the island, he pulled the phone from his pocket and dialed a familiar number. "Dr. Rob, do you have a minute?"

"Wait a minute. *Ah*, how are you, my old fishing buddy. You caught me on my lawn mower cutting for the first time this season. Wouldn't have answered if I hadn't seen you name on the caller ID."

The loud engine silenced and his college roommate came back on the line. "How are you feeling? Is something wrong we need to talk about?"

Concern in his oncologist's voice reassured Grayson. "No, no, I'm fine. I have a hypothetical situation for you, a doctor question.

"I'm listening."

"If someone has amnesia, what do you do? Do you tell them what they're missing or let them work it out on their own?" He repeated for emphasis, "hypothetically speaking."

"Well now, sounds like you're in a real predicament. There are two schools of thought. One says tell'em and the other says not to. How does that help your scenario -- hypothetically speaking, I mean?" Grayson could see his friend smiling across the miles that separated them.

"Good buddy, that's no help at all."

"*Ah*, I wish I could talk longer and ask you more about your hypothetical situation, but I need to get back on the mower. I promised to be finished before noon so I can take the wife out to lunch on my day off," he huffed into the phone. "Now, you take care of yourself and that hypothetical amnesiac. Stay out of trouble." With that, the good doctor hung up.

Grayson looked out across the sound and began walking. After hiking another mile, he reached again for his cell phone and made another call.

FOUR

After Grayson left, Lise pushed the tiredness away and rummaged through the kitchen drawers, looking for mail, magazines, anything with his name on it. She searched his desk, but only found blank notebook paper, pencils and pens. Canvases were stacked in vertical bins along one wall. Some finished; she couldn't read the signature. *Who are you? Odd, I can't decide if it's you or me, I want to know more about.*

She climbed the steps once again to look through the hanging locker trying to find identity, history or interests of her host. She figured him to be in his forties, in spite of his missing hair. It was hard to tell.

Tiredness overcoming her, Lise stripped and pulled back the shower curtain. The claw-footed bathtub offered a tempting retreat from her morning angst. The curtain hung on a stainless steel circle suspended from the ceiling. She fiddled with the old-fashioned fixtures mixing the water until she found the right temperature. When she flipped the flow knob, water flushed into the showerhead.

The hot water stung her skin. She laughed when she caught herself looking for shampoo. Of course, he wouldn't have any. She soaped her hair and body with his pungent soap. After drying off with a deliciously thick towel, she pulled on the same clothes. Lise plowed her fingers through her hair after she hung her towel next to his, straightening them both on the rack. She frowned and adjusted her washcloth to match his. *Everything appears so proper, Grayson. Your house is like a picture from House Beautiful. I noticed there were no mirrors in the bathroom or anywhere else. Are you self-conscious or sensitive about your looks?*

The large four-poster bed with plaid sheets beckoned like open arms. Lise spread back the light-weight quilt that she wrapped up in while looking for clothes. It matched the colors of the sheets and the pale yellow walls. Weary, she climbed onto the bed and pulled up the sheet. The house was definitely a 1940's vintage but there were subtle changes. He had replaced windows and painted walls, but kept a vintage look with the unpainted wide plank floors. Staring up into the skylight, Lise felt her lids grow heavy. A deep sleep pulled her under.

In the dream she was running. Her side ached. She sucked in stale air. She felt stifled. They came crashing in the woods behind her, calling her name. A man and a woman chased her. The older one grabbed her wrist and she pulled away. "No. Go away. Please, leave me alone!" His face faded as the forest closed in on her. Her heart pounded in her ears. She gasped for air.

Lise woke with a shudder and noticed the dark bruise turning from black to brownish-yellow on her arm. She rolled over into the face of the red dog again and frowned. "Well, hello, dog. Do you know who I am or why they're chasing me?"

The dog happily panted back nudging his head under her hand. He hopped onto the bed and rolled on his back. "Casey, no." She didn't know if the dog was allowed on the bed, but he seemed at home. The dog rolled to his side and stretched. "Well, things can't be so bad if I have you for a friend." She rubbed his belly for a moment then scooted to the edge of the bed. Fighting the vertigo, she placed both feet on the floor.

Grayson called from below. "You awake up there? Want to walk around outside? It might help to shake out the cobwebs."

"I'll be down in a minute." She shoved the dog away as she pulled a tie from his wardrobe. *Strange man to keep one tie balled up inside a pair of deck shoes.* She strung it through the belt loops drawing the waistband tighter. She bent over and examined the tiny pearl ring in her navel. *Nice touch. I guess if a lady's going to wake up with a body she doesn't know, this one's pretty good.* She went into the bathroom to splash water on her face. "Come on, dog. Let's not keep the master waiting."

"Did you say something?" Grayson put a canvas bag of groceries on the counter and glanced up at her. "I like the tie." He smiled.

"I thought you said your boat didn't work. How'd you get supplies?" She watched him bite his bottom lip. She was adjusting to the look of him. He wasn't ugly, but the memory of the scars and baldness distracted her.

"No, it's delivered. Never know when she'll show up. A woman who runs a store on the mainland brings them. She and her son fish this area. Need anything? I'll put in an order for you."

"I don't plan to stay long enough to place an order. How often does she come? As soon as I get back to the mainland, wherever that is, I'm sure I can find my way home."

"I don't think so." Grayson put both hands on her shoulders and looked at her eye-to-eye. "Consider staying for awhile. Maybe you'll remember what you forgot. You've said some disturbing things in your sleep. You remember first and then I'll let you go home."

His hands felt warm and gentle on her shoulders. She bit her top lip as she mulled over his proposition.

Grayson made a Boy Scout pledge gesture. "I promise. Casey isn't complaining. You have freedom of my island and all you have to do is get your memory back while letting me paint." He patted the dog's back and opened the screen door. "Come on outside."

She hadn't made up her mind about the stay, but he was right. She rubbed her stomach. "I know I'm unsettled and I'm running, but I don't know why."

He leaned against the screen door enjoying the smell of his soap on her body when she walked by. His body warmed to her closeness. He felt perspiration form on his top lip. “Lise, allow me to give you the grand tour.” He was careful not to call her Annie, her childhood name as he guided her around the house and pointed. “That’s where I catch the rain water. It’s an old cistern but it still works. I painted the PVC that runs along the roof, there. It heats our water, passive solar.”

“Drinking water, too? So, you’ve lived here a while?”

“Yep, on both counts. My grandfather fished, my father fished. I used to fish. When my paintings began to sell, I turned the marketing over to an agent and gallery in town. I moved out here to get away from the stares, the pity, the… I painted before the cancer diagnosis.” He tapped the top of his head. “Maybe the cancer tweaked my artistic talents. I dunno. I’m grateful for the change in career. The hours and the work are a lot easier than pulling crab pots or hauling a net.”

“Did you have formal training?”

“I took a few classes here and there. The brush does the painting. I only hold it.” He smiled, not wanting to brag about his extensive training. “You should be painted.”

“Oh no, buster, I’ve heard that line before.”

“Really, when was that?” he waited.

“I don’t know, but I can’t stay, as pleasant as it is here. I can’t stay. I have a job, a home. I have to go back soon.”

Too bad, in his clothes, she looked like she belonged on his island. “At any rate, stay as long as you want.” The words came out before he had a chance to realize what he conveyed. No woman would be attracted to him or his hairless scarred body to stay with him. He glanced away, swallowing a bitter thought. He scowled but then coughed to revive his good humor. “If you have time I’d like you to sit for me to do a few sketches.”

“We’ll see. Do you have family around here?”

“My father died when I was a teenager, lung cancer. My wife died in an automobile accident. My only partner recently has been the big C-cancer.” His fingers made rabbit ears framing the letter.

“Were you close to your father?” Her eyes narrowed. “I don’t have a good feeling about mine.” Her gaze followed the movement of her toe pushing a cockle shell in the sand.

He spoke softly. “My father and mother gave me all the time that I needed. I see her often, my brother, too. I miss my dad, especially when I do something he taught me.”

He felt she didn’t want to look at him. He consoled himself with her conversation, company and inevitable departure. Swallowing to gain control of his disappointment, he said, “Only my dog and me here, now.” He quickly added, “Tell me more about your family.”

“I have a brother. Oh! That was a trick question.” She smiled broadly. “I do have a brother. I can see him, but not anything around him. He’s laughing about something. She pulled a strand of red hair away from her face to stare at it. “He has sandy brown hair.”

“A pity, yours is beautiful.” He remembered the brother, a bully and a self-centered boy who became a self-indulgent young man. It was a good thing she didn't act like Ted Basnight. Maybe she really lost her memory. If he had her family, he would have wanted to escape them, too.

She stopped walking and held her head with both hands. "It's no use. I don't remember. He seems older…" She frowned. "You'd probably be about his age."

Ted and he were the same age, fifteen years senior to Lise. "It'll come. Don't try so hard. It'll come." When he reached across her back, nudging her forward, he felt a warm buzz jump between them. She must have felt it too, because she blushed. He couldn't believe he felt attracted to Ted's freckled-faced kid sister who'd grown up.

Four small horses ambled around a shed. "These are my ponies, but I don't own them. There are others on the island, but these like my company." He reached in his pocket and pulled out several matted brown clumps. "Horse cookies, made with molasses and grass. Here, you feed them." He watched as Lise's hands moved along their bristly chins and rubbed their velvet noses.

Lise tugged at the mane. "They're shedding their winter coats."

Soft fur clumped in patches along their sides. A mare, heavy with foal, watched from the shadow of an oak tree. Lise ran her hand down the dark line on the dun's back and then tickled behind his ears.

Grayson imagined her hand running down his back. The familiarity drew a damp sweat under his shirt. "I have chickens, too." He wiped his mouth self-consciously.

"So you have a family: ponies, chickens, a dog, and now me." She cleared her throat. "Where am I?

He pointed in several directions as he talked. "North Carolina sticks out into the Atlantic Ocean. On the bottom of the crescent is this island, Harrold's Island. The Cape Fear River isn't far away." He turned her, looked her full in the face. "Welcome to my island. I'd rather you not try to leave until you regain your memory."

"Ok, I have a good feeling about this place. You have a deal. There's something about it I can't quite pull out of this head." She tapped her temple. "But I trust you -- for some unknown reason. You're right, how can I leave if I have no idea where I'm going?"

He studied her face to see if her facial expression matched her words. Maybe he would stretch her time limit to a full week. He was relieved she agreed to stay, because he knew if he let her go back, no one would believe she stole a million dollars and forgot where she left it.

FIVE

After dinner that evening, Lise went outside to sit in a white porch rocker. The tightness in her stomach released as she inhaled deeply. “You’re not an entertaining host, Grayson. All afternoon I’ve tried to be interested in what you’re doing, but you ignored me. Are you avoiding talking to me?”

“I told you when I paint, I paint. I have to finish this series before the end of the month, so don’t try to interrupt me when I work.” He took another step closer to the back porch after feeding his animals.

“Well, I’m sorry to be such a problem. I’m here trying to find answers, remember. The day is over. Can’t we sit and talk now, leisurely without me drawing your ire?”

He grumbled a response.

“Why two?” She pointed back and forth between the two chairs. “Why does a man living alone have two rocking chairs on his porch?” She offered a tentative smile. He looked for a moment as if he were chewing marbles.

“You pry. Don’t you know how to sit, be still and be quiet?”

"I don't think so. Whatever I was, I had to be doing something, busy, moving. My Type-A personality is emerging. I guess we're different about that. I've watched you today. You can sit or stand and stare, nothing else. Just "be" for ten minutes or more without moving." She tapped on the armrest to resist saying anything contrary.

He held up two fingers. "My grandparents always had two chairs on this porch. I get company too."

"*Ah.*" She watched him climb the steps, wash his hands in the outside sink and pull a rocker into the shade of the overhang. A gnat buzzed her head and she fanned it away. "Talk to me."

"Every day gets longer." He pulled his cap lower on his head shading his eyes. "It's getting warmer and the humidity will follow. When I was a kid, it never bothered me. When I moved back here, after the chemo, I could barely move. I learned how to relax, sit and do nothing -- as you say. You should try it now that you have the time."

"Right, me, without anything to do. Ok. I have my homework, Mr. Teacher." She fanned her hand again at the nagging insects around her face.

"We had a lot of rain last month and with the warmth, the mosquitoes will be hatching. When the wind blows from the east, like now, the no-see'ems and mosquitoes come."

"It has been warm today. So this is an east wind." Talking about the weather seemed safer. She pursed her lips. "I almost feel like Dorothy in the Wizard of Oz, trying to get back home, but I can't find the yellow brick road. You're not the helpful lion or scarecrow." As she thought about that, she concluded he was more like a lion, roaring and growling at her, as if he'd never been around a woman. "Are you more like the tin man or the lion?"

She broke his reverie. "What?"

Lise took a patient deep breath. "I said, 'are you more like the tin man or the lion?' You know in the *Wizard of Oz*. Maybe I have my stories confused. Or is this story more like *Beauty and the Beast*? You won't let me go home and you growl."

His eyes narrowed. "I know I'm not the brainless scarecrow. You figure out the rest." He sat silently watching the sky. His bottom lip twitched when she mentioned *The Beauty and the Beast* fairytale, but she continued with her Oz-talk.

"Maybe you're the Wizard! At least Dorothy knew where home was." Her nervousness was mounting. "Where do you think I'm from?" He didn't respond. "I'm chattering again. Sorry." She pulled an invisible zipper across her mouth and sat trying not to interrupt his thoughts.

The sun set across the island, throwing red and orange streaks through piles of purple cumulous clouds. Marsh hens and crickets serenaded them as night fell on the island. She began to understand his attraction to this place. It was beautiful. Shrugging off the evening's mantle of peace, she broke their silence. "So what do you do out here when it gets dark?"

He leaned forward resting his elbows on his knees. "Usually, *I* go to bed."

Lise gulped. "Whoa! We need to talk about that."

Grayson stood, kicked his shoes off, leaving them on the porch and entered the house. Lise brushed off her bare feet before following him.

Blowing out the match after lighting a lantern, Grayson said, "Yep, it's time for bed." He left the lamp on the kitchen countertop and rounded the table.

"Wait. I only see one bed and your couch is too short for sleepovers. Where do you sleep if I'm in your bed?"

He turned. "*I* sleep in *my* bed. I've never had complaints about sleeping arrangements before." His mouth widened, creasing his smooth cheeks.

She thought he probably had regular romps in bed with women vying for an artist's attention. Lise huffed at the thought of anyone else sharing his bed.

In the dim kitchen, she felt his eyes probe her face. She stared at the space where the collar of his shirt stood open around his neck. She could almost feel the pulse in his neck thumping out at her. She hesitated and looked away.

"You didn't seem to mind it before. It's a big bed." He waited.

"We both slept in that bed? Together? Last night?" "I was naked!"

"So was I." He stared back. "I'll pull on some shorts if that bothers you. Casey may hop up but push him away."

"I don't think that I want to sleep with you or your dog," Lise squawked.

"See, that's the thing. It's *my* house, *my* island and *my* bed. You don't have to make up your mind." Grayson climbed the stairs and his dog followed. He tossed back his final words of the evening. "You can sleep with both of us."

Lise heard the water running overhead. He'd smell like his spicy soap and be warm from his shower. She pictured water running down his chest then plowed her mind in a different direction. It had been a while since she had slept with a man and knew about it.

She blew out the flickering lantern and felt her way toward the couch. Now she remembered the candles by the bathroom sink. *He showers by candlelight. How charming.*

The smell of kerosene followed her to the living room where she stretched out on the floor. It seemed his easel's long legs took up a third of the room. A couch cushion beneath her head, Lise lay on her back. The water cut off upstairs and the floor creaked as he walked across the room. The cool night air made her yearn for that quilt on the bottom of his bed. Lise remembered the softness and its warmth. She groaned. *His wife probably made it. His quilt, his floor, his rules.*

As she turned on her shoulder, pain shot down her arm. *Humph.* She tossed the pillow back on the couch and crawled onto the double cushion loveseat. The wooden arms banged her head or trapped her feet depending on which way she shifted. No matter which way she turned, her feet hung over. She pivoted to her side arching her neck and knees into a fetal position. The kitchen clock ticked loudly now as she listened to it. Outside a horse snuffled in the dark, but the crickets were quiet. Lise stood finally and stepped out to the porch thinking the night air might soothe her mind, but mosquitoes drove her inside.

Exhausted, she crept up the stairs, her fingers feeling the grooves along the wallboards. At the top of the steps, she paused getting her bearings. Her ears picked up Grayson's quiet breathing on the far side of the bed. As she eased onto the bed and pulled up the sheet, Casey raised his head. She pushed the dog onto the floor where he whined, but flopped down. As soon as Lise wiggled into place and plumped up her pillow, sleep came and so did the nightmare.

Her feet pounded on the pavement. People shouted for her. She dived behind a building. A chain link fence scratched her arms and face as she shimmied over it. Panic! Cars passed on a nearby highway. Sirens wailed. "I didn't mean to kill him." Fighting the sheets, heart pounding, Lise jerked herself awake. Names melted along with her dream, replaced by the smell of new rain blowing through the doorway. Rain tapped on the skylight overhead calming her. A curtain flapped against the sill. She turned over still listening as her racing heart slowed.

***

Grayson's eyes flew open, but he didn't move. Her shout rang in his ears. *My God*, he thought, *what kind of woman has she become? Why would she steal? Who did she kill?*

He had seen her lying unconscious, without clothes, but preferred the constantly moving, talkative version, who wandered his home that day. She'd pick up things and put them down a few inches away from where he preferred. She straightened the knives on their rack and spoons in his drawer. Her slender fingers were always touching, smoothing, adjusting. His mind retraced how she looked -- her pierced navel ring, the way the shirt hugged her breasts above her neat knot, her neck, and all that coppery hair that fell into place despite the breeze.

He lost touch with her family years before, after winning an art school competition. Leaving Savannah where he studied art, he spent several years in Europe where he backpacked and sketched. He'd heard she took over the family business after her father died suddenly. Her mother was probably still the helpless belle dependant on Anne and her legal advisors. The mother had secluded herself whenever they visited the coast, staying behind the walls and glass. He heard she had a fondness for booze. The Basnight family came from money and made more money in their Charlotte firm. How did Annie end up on his island?

He was no longer the poor fisherman's son who sold bait at his father's shop. His new money bought him a home in Southport, but lately, he preferred his grandparents' house. If her old man were still alive, he'd continue to scoff at the fisherman's son. If he wasn't good enough to be the son's playmate, he certainly wasn't fit to be sleeping with his daughter.

Why did he enjoy her company now, though he tried not to let it show? She'd never stay when she remembered. His grief for his lost wife had shrunk to a ripple in his heart, but Annie's long legs, her busy fingers, the way she flipped her hair when it fell on her face, her lips when she pursed them, all these sensual traits stirred his interest.

As he pondered the situation, his toes began to tingle - another minor annoyance from his medications. He stretched his legs to the bottom of the bed, moving slowly. Annie sat up. He froze, but she rolled on her side away from him. Her breathing returned to normal. He punched his pillow back under his head and willed sleep to return.

They both slept quieter the rest of the night.

SIX

Lise awoke the next morning to a warm body curled against her back. She froze.

Her anger grew into a slow boil. *Darn him. He's supposed to stay on his side of the bed!* His breath tickled the back of her neck, but when he licked her shoulder, she jumped.

The bed was empty except for a startled Casey. Embarrassed, she roughed the dog's fur, and then went over to the bureau in search of a clean tee shirt. *Going without underwear can be habit forming. I feel a little naughty.* Having rummaged through his clothes previously, she realized he also went without. *Definitely interesting.* She showered and dressed.

She tromped down the steps to find Grayson finishing his breakfast. "It's occurred to me that I have no underwear," she announced. "I hate to be an ungrateful castaway, but I need a few essentials. How about we go to town and let me get some things?"

He placed a tea bag with a cup of hot water on the table when she sat down and scraped out his final spoonful of cereal without answering. Deciding to be patient, for once, Lise quietly dunked her teabag while he stacked his dishes.

He rolled a pencil and fluttered a piece of paper at her. “Make a list of what you need. I don’t mind you not wearing underwear but if you’re going to fuss, we’ll get you some. Granny pants, tidy whities or thong?”

Ignoring his taunt, Lise reached for the pencil.

“There’s probably other girly things you’ll need.” He pushed a bowl her way and pointed to the drawer where she found a spoon. “Want some cereal? There are fresh blueberries.”

“I’m not asking for a sixty-four thousand dollar shopping spree, just the bare essentials.” She smiled, hoping he’d return one.

His chair scraped the floor as he rose. “I won’t be taking you to town, Lise. Whoever is looking for you may not be friendly.” He turned with concern in his eyes, “Do you remember any of your dreams?” He propped his hip against the counter. “You’re running from something or someone. You said you killed someone.” He paused. “Did you?”

She felt heat rise to her face. “I don’t know.”

“Would it help you to know that *I’m* not afraid of you? Nothing I’ve seen from you while you’ve been here makes me afraid of you.” He tossed the hand towel on the sink drain board. “I’ll leave you to finding your lost past. I’ll work around you.”

She waggled her finger to catch his attention. “Now, see, we have a problem, because I don’t know if I need you --

to work around me. I need for you to help me to solve my memory problem."

"I think it's best if you solve your memory problem, as you call it, on your own." He shrugged, reached for another hat and walked out the door. "You don't need me to tell you a thing. I'll see you later. There are some books stacked by the couch. Read for a while. Take your mind off remembering so hard. It's time for my walk."

"You are a strange man," Lise murmured under her breath. When she had washed her cereal bowl, she found a sack with "Lise" written on it. He'd sketched an island tree and sea grass on the side of the bag. *Nice.* Inside were a new toothbrush, a comb and toothpaste, as well as other goodies. *Suddenly the morning seems a bit like Christmas.* She scurried up the steps to break open her new treasures.

Later, she found him mixing his paints with a small putty knife. He wore a Cubs baseball cap turned backwards on his head. His unbuttoned denim shirt hung open. Sleeves torn off at the seam revealed lean muscled arms. The waistline of his jeans gripped his body beneath his navel. She figured he lost weight during his cancer, but his stomach and chest looked like the cover of an erotic paperback. *Keep your mind on your current memory problem, Lise,* she warned herself.

As she watched Grayson dab color, trees grew, blossoms twined along a split rail fence and a brook appeared. She drew closer to look over his shoulder. Sunlight warmed her back as she peered at two snapshots clipped above his canvas. She saw that he combined the best elements of both pictures into one painting.

She moved closer until she could feel the heat from his body. "It's beautiful. The water actually looks like it moves."

He never took his eyes off the painting. "Good. I had to work at that. Would you mind stepping back? You're in my light." He sipped at his coffee.

"Sorry." She backed away, her shadow disappearing from his canvas. "By the way, thanks for the goodies. Where is it, what you're painting?"

He ignored her thanks. "This is a place I visit when I'm in the North Carolina mountains."

"Where?"

"It's between Banner Elk and Valle Crucis. My wife and I used to go there. We took these pictures years ago." His brush hand hesitated in the air. "Ever been there?"

"I don't think so." Lise felt uncomfortable at the mention of his wife." I'm sorry for your loss."

He grunted his acknowledgement.

"How long has it been?"

He mixed another batch of green for the distant mountains, used a smaller brush, took a deep breath and let it out slowly. "She died Christmas Eve - three years, two months and ten days ago. It's March now."

Uncomfortable about where the conversation was leading, Lise dropped to the couch and picked up a book. She read for a while, but her eyes drifted toward his host again. As he moved in front of his canvas, his bare feet stepped back and forth in a private dance. She noticed his second toe was longer than his big toe. *He has clam digger toes, just like mine.* She held out her feet and smiled comparing toes.

He bent down and then to the side, painting, dipping his brush, swirling colors on the five foot square canvas.

"How long does it take you to do a painting this size?"

He growled, "You're breaking my train of thought." He paused then huffed out a breath. "My wife had her own pastimes and knew not to interrupt me." He continued to paint, dabbing color, switching brushes until he held five in his hand. "She was a fabric artist. She made custom clothes, quilts, shawls and things for boutiques."

So Grayson's wife did make the quilt on his bed.

He fell silent again, but his brushes continued to jab at different spots on the canvas, as if they had their own energy. "Sometimes it takes years to get it right. Sometimes in a couple of days, I have the whole thing roughed in. It depends. I go back to a painting months later and re-do something." Another easel at the side of the room held a painting. Lise guessed it was drying.

She walked to the vertical bins, built along one wall, where various canvases leaned against one another. Pulling each out, she studied the paintings. Spring meadows burst with flowers. Somber misty roads wound through woods. Half were deep-forested mountains and the other half marshes, boats, ponies or children playing.

“Do you have children?” She judged him no older than his forties, in spite of his baldness.

“*Hmmm,* what?” He stepped over and shoved the paintings back in the bin. He growled, “Do you mind?”

“I asked you if you had children.”

“No.” He rubbed a hand over his chin smearing a fleck of green paint with his hand. “We wanted children, but it never happened. How about you?” He wiped his hand on his jeans.

“No.” She was sure. The answer came from somewhere deep inside. Lise pulled another painting from the bin of canvases. "These are good. Better than most, I imagine. Are you famous? I mean I don't know any artists that aren't dead." She frowned and pouted her lips as she studied them. He didn't turn to watch her as she shuffled through the stack. "You make what a couple of thousand if you can sell one?"

Grayson grunted once more and picked up another brush without answering.

“Do I have children?” There he was again prodding her mind with his questions. Something tugged at her heart for a moment, but no face appeared. “I’d love a houseful of children. We’d be a real family, not like mine. Oh!” The thought popped out of her mouth. “I must not come from a happy home.” She tapped her chest confidently and nodded. “I’m going to have lots of children. That’s what I want,” she spoke with conviction.

“*Humph,*” he mumbled. “I wish you luck. Speaking of which, have you had any more morning sickness, nausea?”

"No. I can't be pregnant. It was probably the sea water and shock of being so cold, like you said." She turned to face him. She tried to recall a caress, a kiss, the feel of a man's touch. Feeling the heat rise in her face, she dropped her chin and looked at her stomach. The pearl seemed to smile back at her. "Would you mind if Casey and I go for a walk while you paint?" To cover her embarrassment, she added. "I don't want to be a bother."

"Go, please!" He spoke loudly. She rushed to the kitchen, but he called after her, "Take a hat. They're behind the back door. The sun can get mean in early spring and surprise you with a burn." *Great. Children, she wants children.* He wasn't sure if he could have children after the chemotherapy.

Could she become interested in a hairless man covered with scars not knowing if he could father a child? His fear of recurring cancer had shaped the image of himself into a grotesque man, with a shadowy future. There was even a nagging problem about Pauli. Was his brother's slowness an inherited trait?

He put down his brush and peered through the double row of louvered windows as she walked up a sand dune. Casey jumped at her, teasing. She laughed and tugged at a stick the dog found. Lise's bothersome presence tugged at Grayson.

Annie-Lise, Grayson-Eric, his mind was already beginning to get used to the names changing. He shook his head. What was he thinking? She was a bother, an annoyance, from a different world. Why had she come back after so many years? Had she really killed someone after the embezzlement? Had she faked the lost memory? He growled like the beast from her fairy tale. Perhaps he should turn her over her to the police and be done with it.

SEVEN

A cool breeze sent goose bumps along Lise's arms. Her feet squished in the sand. Except for the fact that she didn't have any idea who she was, she felt great. Her stomach no longer clutched at her insides. Extreme pleasure flushed though her body.

She trailed the dog to the shore. With a north wind blowing across the island, the ocean laid flat, barely rippling against the shore. She swung a driftwood staff as she paced along, feet crunching on soft sand and sea fragments. She stooped to brush off the shells.

"Going to have to get myself some shoes." Talking aloud gave her confidence. "Casey, my good man, tell me about that fellow you live with." The dog stopped and perked up his ears. "I'd like to know more about him! Is he a beast of a man or am I just not his type?"

Casey barked and bounced up to her, his coat dark from salt water.

"*Uh-oh*, boss man's not going to be happy if I bring you home all wet."

An hour later, she figured they had walked about four miles. She still had energy. “Come on. Let’s see what’s up there.”

She jogged up the dune with the dog trotting beside her. A thicket of trees and a small lake blocked the view of one end of the island. Sand dunes stretched across the horizon in the other direction. Lise recognized the trees and lake from one of Grayson’s paintings.

A herd of ponies grazed at the edge of the lake. One lifted his head, eyeing her approach. “It’s ok. I’m not going to hurt you.” The horse kept the distance between them as she approached. She stopped. He stopped. She walked. He walked a few steps away. “So that’s the way it is, eh. Well, if I bring horse cookies, I bet you’ll let me come closer.”

The horse snuffled a response and trotted over to the others, nudging them with a whinny. They trotted towards the woods, eventually disappearing into the tangled oaks.

Lise hopped through reeds crossing a dry lake bed. Cracks in the dried mud reminded her of smashed eggshells. She balled her fists and saw distinct biceps muscles. She felt her legs and hard stomach. “I must work out. Ouch!” A sandspur embedded itself in the tough sole of her foot. Lise plucked the burr and flicked it into the breeze. Casey trotted up and licked her foot. She scratched his neck. “Up to your old trick again, aren’t you?” She sat in the sand and the dog offered his belly for a rub that Lise obliged.

Lise finally stood and turned toward the north side of the island. The long fetch from the sound sent ripples washing over reeds and marsh. Her feet sank in the mud and she struggled to pull free. Realizing the danger of the sucking sand, Lise groped toward higher ground and eventually crossed back over a grassy area towards where she supposed the house stood. The dog hesitated and then accompanied her gleefully until a wide band of water cut a zigzag through their sand-land path.

Warm water covered the trough's squishy mud bottom. After Lise's cold walk through the ocean's tide, the warmth felt good on her bare feet. She rolled the pant legs up further. When the water reached her thighs, she thought about taking off her jeans and holding her clothes over her head. "What the heck. I'm already wet. Come on, Casey."

The dog hesitated before plunging in. Lise fell when the water dropped off another foot. By then, they were both groping for their footing. Relieved when she righted herself, she stood and raced the dog to the dry sand. They climbed another dune, but nothing looked familiar. She looked down at Casey, who was gnawing on his coat.

"You know which way is home." Salt air blew from the sound, so she figured they were north of the house. "Go home. Go find Grayson. Go!"

She shooed the dog and he loped in the opposite direction than she would have taken. Lise followed his tracks over the next hill, relieved to see the dark solar pipes on the tin roof. When the dog returned, Lise said, "Well, I wasn't too far off. Don't mention to him I was lost."

The Irish setter lunged up on her with wet sandy paws. "Uh-oh, the Master is not going to like you are wet *and* smelling like something dead. *Yuck*, what did you roll in?"

She walked down towards the house and stumbled upon a rusted oil drum filled with burned debris. Among the feather of fine ash, she found a leather strap and buckle. *This could have been a purse.* Lise used her stick to dig in the remains, but found nothing more. She tucked that fact away as she headed down to the house. *Did he burn my purse and all my identification?* A tingle rose from the base of her skull along with her uneasiness.

***

Grayson was pleased with the progress of his paintings. Josie, his agent would be delighted. Lise energized his painting. His brush fogged in clouds. More birds and flowers sprouted. The colors washed brilliantly across the canvas-backed dunes and sky. She brought a seldom felt warmth to his body. He focused on two canvases side by side, a progression he never finished. One sunset flowed between the two works and an oak grove grew across the edges from one to another. He stopped only to make a sandwich, which he ate while he walked out on the porch. *Where are they? They should be coming soon. Surely, she's hungry.* His eyes scanned the circumference of his yard as he brushed crumbs from his hands. Seeing nothing, he returned to his work.

He put his brush down finally when he heard barking and went to the back door. It was then that he noticed her stirring up his burn site. Grayson wondered if everything had burned completely. Sheepishly, he remembered burning papers and envelopes, anything with his name printed on it, along with his old fishing tote. Would she be suspicious? Surely, she'd never recognize the old canvas bag from when she was a girl, not in her state of mind, but he wasn't certain.

He put a paintbrush into a jar to soak with several others and went out to greet them. "Welcome home, stranger."

Her face was a blank as she approached. "We're back," she said, adding an edge he hadn't noticed before.

"The two of you are soaking wet!" he said, trying not to stare at the outline of her breasts and nipples beneath the damp shirt or the way the soaked jeans hugged her long legs. "The hose is over there beneath the shower head." His nose picked up the foul odor and he grimaced. "Did Casey find something to roll in? I'll bring out soap, towels and something for you to change into.

Grayson watched from the porch as she washed and rinsed the dog. He called to Casey only after the dog had shaken fine spray, a third time, over Lise. "I'll dry him from here on. You go ahead and shower."

She took the robe and towel and then stepped behind the thread-bare shower curtain at the corner of his house. When his grandparents lived in the house, it was their only shower. He added the one upstairs the past year.

Grayson watched as Lise pulled the shower curtain against the side of the house. She stepped under the hot water spray, keeping on her clothes until all the mud and sand washed free. When she pulled off the wet jeans, she lost her balance. Her hand grabbed at the plumbing fixture. He hid a grin in his shoulder when she peeked out at him.

As he dried off the dog, Grayson couldn't keep his eyes away. The wet shower curtain clung to her bare bottom every time she bent over. He remembered those hips. He thought she was dead when he untangled her from that slip of cloth. Now that life thrived beneath her smooth skin, her curves bewitched him. Judging from the hardness growing inside his jeans, he didn't have to worry about impotency any longer. He was glad the dog stood between them when she approached.

The seersucker robe clung to her damp body. Her breasts peeped out as she stooped to wipe her feet on her towel. "Take a picture. It lasts longer," she sneered never looking up. "You've seen me without clothes, Grayson, but I do have a modicum of modesty left." She grabbed the front of her robe.

"Sorry, Lise, I'm a man. We always look."

Lips pressed together, she searched his face and then hugged the robe closer as she slipped in the door. Her mixed feelings began to churn in her mind. Lise heard Grayson talk to the dog as she poured herself a glass of juice in the kitchen.

"Well, we're going to have to be more careful in what we do and say from now on. You behave and don't get us into trouble again, okay?" The dog whined his appreciation for the rubdown.

When she finished her juice, she went up to the bedroom to find two Wal-Mart bags on the bed. One contained shorts, long pants, and several tee shirts. A belt and sunglasses were in the second. *The clothes are my size. Where did he get them? How could he get them so quickly?* She searched for a sales receipt.

She shivered as she remembered a movie from the 1960's, the "Butterfly Collector." An eccentric man kidnapped the woman of his dreams and kept her until she died trying to escape. Her fear turned to anger the more she thought of it. *What is he hiding? What happened to my memory?*

Lise pulled on the trousers and knit shirt. She hung up her towel and robe before she went to find him. "Grayson, I want answers. How long have you known me? Where did you get these clothes? How did you know what size?"

He was replacing a fence post and turned shoving the blade of his shovel into the ground. "I really don't know you." He pointed with a finger. "You looked the size of my wife. Ella, the woman who lives on the mainland brought them over earlier while you were on your walk. I told her about you when she brought the groceries. She said, by the way, no one was murdered recently."

"Take me to the mainland."

"I can't do that."

"When is this Ella coming again?" Her throat ached in frustration. "What kind of man are you to keep me against my will?"

"You said you didn't mind staying." He took a deep breath. "What got you so riled? Before, you said you wanted to stray until you remembered." He shook his head in annoyance. "I never know when Ella will come. Between running her bait shop, taking care of her son and fishing, she comes when she has the time." He removed his hat and wiped his head in his elbow. "I don't know who's chasing you. I don't know who you killed. How can I make you believe me?"

He ran his hand over his head then realized she was staring, horrified at either hearing his words or seeing the scars on his scalp. "Oh, sorry, you must hate looking at me." He replaced his hat. "I don't understand you. One moment you seem content to be here and the next, you fly into a rage. You're a lot like the shifting sands around this island."

She hissed and stomped her foot in frustration.

"You're tired and probably hungry after your walk. Come on. I'll fix you something."

Grayson's explanations seemed feasible. She knew he could have tried anything when she was unconscious. He was ashamed of his scars. He couldn't help having them and he appeared to have won his battle with cancer.

Food? Why was he changing the subject? "I'm not looking for a picnic! I want to go home." She clinched her fists and beat on his chest. His image blurred through tears that fell on her new shirt. She tried to pull away, but he held her firmly. "You've done this before! I remember you holding my wrists."

"You fought me when I found you. I'm sorry if I hurt you."

"Who are you and why am I here?"

A stony face stared back into hers. With no emotion, he dropped her wrists and stuck his hands in his pockets. "I've told you all I can."

She picked up the shovel and lifted it over her head.

He turned, catching it. "If you hurt or kill me, then what?" He leaned toward her. "Is this what you did? Did someone make you angry enough to kill him? Do you want someone to find me dead and you ranting about the island? Where would you go? Who could you trust?"

Something clicked in her mind, a glimpse of him long ago. He was sitting on a step and talking with her. It was Grayson! He wasn't her enemy. He was explaining something to her. The image vanished as quickly as it came. With slumped shoulders, she dropped the shovel, turned and walked into the house. "I don't know. I'm sorry. You've been the perfect gentleman since I woke up the first day, but," She pointed to a dip between the dunes. "tell me about that burn pile over there."

"Once a week I burn my trash that can't be recycled. What is the matter with you?" His arms went out in exasperation. "What has that got to do with anything? Don't think I haven't thought about ways to help you remember. I don't know what you were up to before you came here." He shook his head. "I can't read your mind either."

"I don't know what's going on." Lise held her head and squeezed it. Touching the tender spot on her forehead, she winced. She scuffed up the steps and into the house, dropping on the couch. She leaned her head back and stared at the ceiling. She moaned, "What am I going to do?"

"You could eat." Lise heard Grayson enter the kitchen. Dishes and silverware settled on the table and he was making something.

She smelled tuna fish and heard him pouring tea. He pulled out his chair and called her. "Late lunch or early supper is on the table. Come join me."

Clinching her teeth, she followed his voice into the kitchen.

"I don't know if you take sugar in your ice tea or not."

"I don't know, either. That's what is so frustrating. I remembered you or thought it was you. You were younger with a pony tail and plaid flannel shirt. We were sitting on some porch steps."

"You think it was me?" His top lip disappeared under his bottom one. "Anything else?"

She shook her head, wondering if it was Grayson. She gulped down the tea and ate the sandwich. "Thank you for dinner." She rinsed out her glass and set her plate into the sink, running sudsy water over it. "I apologize for my outburst. I'm going up to take a nap and I won't be any further bother to you this evening." She grabbed a book and trudged up the steps. "Ouch!"

“What?”

“Nothing, I must have cut my foot during my walk. Do you have a Band-Aid?”

“Look on the top shelf, cabinet, in the bathroom. Need any help?”

“No, I don’t need any help.”

“Better have you shod before you take off on the island again. When I see Ella, I’ll have her bring over some shoes next trip.”

“You may not be able to afford keeping me, mister.” She stood at the top of the steps looking down.

“Don’t worry about it. You may want to put some peroxide or something on your foot.”

“Yeah, yeah.”

The medicine cabinet revealed a shelf of over-the-counter medications next to pills zip-locked in small clear plastic bags. *There is no name, no doctor and no date on any of these.* She bandaged her cut. Hopping to the bed, she threw back the covers. For the first time she noticed the round porthole at the roof’s peak. It cast an oblong shadow on the opposite wall. Lise watched it move across the room as she read and then heavy lidded, she slipped beneath the covers to sleep.

She slept through the evening and into the night, without dreaming this time. When she awoke the next morning, her arm was around Casey’s neck. The dog waited patiently for her to finish her shower. When she couldn’t find Grayson, she climbed the dune behind the pony shed. Grayson was talking with someone in a boat. Lise ran towards them, but the boat backed out before she could reach it.

The stocky driver wore a wide-brimmed hat and overalls with a tee shirt. *It must be Ella.* The boater lit a cigarette and threw the match overboard. Following a muffled cough, she turned the boat and was gone.

"I want to go home! Why can't I remember?" Lise spun in her tracks and raced back to the house. She pulled bread, eggs, lettuce, tomato and mayonnaise and filled a glass with milk from the refrigerator. When he walked in, she was frying an egg. "I'll cook my own meals from now on. I hate to keep putting you out of your way. I hate this not knowing."

He watched as she fixed a fried egg sandwich with lettuce and tomato. A smiled lingered on his face. "You like fried egg sandwiches."

"Yes. I like fried egg sandwiches. I used to take them to school in a brown paper sack for lunch." Another chink fell into place in her mind. "I see kids in a school cafeteria and windows, lots of windows."

He poured himself another cup of coffee and sat down in front of her. "You are starting to recall your childhood?"

"I remember my school." Lise swallowed, never taking her gaze from his face. "I wore my jeans rolled up a couple of turns. I had a favorite plaid shirt, but I can't remember last week or what I was doing before I came here." She tried picturing him with hair, long and short, black, brown or blond. "You had wavy hair, didn't you? It was longer than other boys wore it," she guessed.

"Do you remember that? Do you see me as I was? Hair on my head and arms?" He ran his hand up his smooth arm, "a human dynamo out trying to change the world. Or was I wearing a suit and tie?"

He had a nice smile, good teeth. "I'm speculating. Nope, I don't see you with any clothes on." She blushed at her faux pas. "I mean I don't see you at all. Well, it was you on the porch with me. You had a ponytail. There were cement block steps and a red sign."

"Guessing is good. Okay, I'll help some. I knew you a long time ago."

"What? You said you didn't know me."

"I said I don't know you now. It was twenty years ago. You were a child. The last time I saw you, you were a teenager."

"Why didn't you tell me this before?"

"I did some research on amnesia and thought I shouldn't tell you anything. You need to work it out in your own mind."

"YOU DID RESEARCH! What does that mean? How come you thought you didn't have to say anything about this to me?" She fumed.

"Easy, now, don't be angry. I thought it was best, but that hasn't gone too well. I've decided to give you little hints. I even consulted a doctor about it."

She scoffed, "How did you do that, carrier seagull?"

"I have my ways. That's not your problem. Your problem, Lise, is to remember who you are and how you got here. Once you do that, you're free to go."

"Did I live here?"

"No. Some things I'll tell you, but I want you to remember. How would you know that I was telling you the truth? Would you believe me?"

She licked the inside of her wrist where some egg yolk dropped.

"You've liked fried egg sandwiches since you were a girl. Your family used to come here on vacations. I knew your brother. Not here, there, on the mainland." He pointed west.

"Are we going to play a guessing game until I remember everything I need to know? This is so one-sided." She studied his face again as her anger cooled. "Do I see a hint of hair growing under your 'Life is Good' hat? You have hair," she touched the top of her ear, "right here."

His hand went up on the wrong side of his face, "There's a bit of stubble. I haven't shaved in days. You've kept me too busy. It's ragged when it grows back. I decided not to be bothered so, I shave off everything. I guess there is some. A few more testosterone boosts like those I've felt lately and my entire body will be covered by hair within the week. You're to blame, you know."

Smirking she said, "*Ah-ha*! Glad to hear I have some effect on you. I thought you were the heartless tin man the first day, then an angry beast. Sorry about that."

"Never mind. Is your temper tantrum over? Are we friends again? What do you want to do today? I don't want you to feel like a prisoner."

"I do, sort of. I'm a prisoner of my empty mind." She crossed her eyes and made a face, sticking out her tongue.

"Now don't give up on yourself. I'm sorry you're so haunted by a forgotten past. I thought you'd remember it all by now." He felt the bristles on his ear again.

"Well, I suggest, if I'm such a bother, you have that Ella take me over there." She pointed out the window over the sink.

He finished washing the frying pan and turned from the sink to get her plate and glass. "No. I don't like the things you say in your sleep. Something else worries me. Are you sure that -- oh never mind." He turned away from her face and looked out the window. "How about if we go fishing or we can..." He threw down the dish rag and rushed out the door.

She stood up to see where he was going.

"I like to fish. Hey, Grayson, I remember. I like to fish!"

EIGHT

The mare was foaling. Lise stood, fascinated, as Grayson approached the mare carefully, talking and stroking the horse. One lone leg and a head appeared in a stream of water. He cooed to the new mama, talking her through the ordeal, running his hands over her as he worked his way around. The horse leaned against the shed, her head down. Lise could see her sides as she breathed in and shuddered. He lifted the mare's tail and ran his arm inside the birth canal. Lise guessed he was checking to see if anything was tangled around the baby horse's neck.

He continued to talk to the mare, comforting her, telling her what a good mother she was. Awed by the scene unfolding, Lise watched the horse's ears flick back and forth listening as Grayson ran his hands over her, congratulating her on her baby. The mare arched again, flushing out the colt and afterbirth. Grayson stood aside as she sniffed her baby and began licking him.

Lise marveled at his gentleness, his confidence, his caring. *He does have a heart and feelings, unlike Oz's Tin*

Man. His deliberate actions and words consoled the new mother and cheered Lise. "This is a new side of you that appeals to me, Grayson."

"Does it? Interesting." He returned to the porch, soaped his arms and hands and rinsed them. "How about that? I'm a new granddaddy!"

"You've done that before."

"Yes. It happens every spring."

"So, you're a granddaddy, before I'm a mother. I'm disappointed somehow, but happy for you. Is it a boy or girl?"

"A boy, but don't be sad. We need to celebrate. No working today. Let's sit on the porch until he's walking. I can take a break." Grayson disappeared past her and returned with a sketch book. She blinked away her tears and listened as charcoal skittered across his page.

By early afternoon, the colt was standing taking his first steps, and looking for breakfast. "Ain't life grand?" Grayson held up his sketch pad to show Lise his drawings.

She shuffled though his sketches while he leaned back, eyes closed in his chair. The first few were of the colt and his mother, but she was startled to see a face staring back at her on the last pages. "Is this me? Is this what I look like?"

"I think so."

"Not very pretty, am I? I mean, I'm not looking for compliments, but without a mirror I don't know what I look like." She looked at the black and white face peering back at her. "Who are you, girl?" He'd drawn as she watched the colt. Lise's eyes full of wonder, a hint of a smile on her face.

"I think you have a very attractive face, Lise." His eyelids fluttered over his closed eyes as he answered her.

"Do I have freckles?"

"You used to and you do have them now." His hands went to her face. He brushed across her cheek and nose with his thumb, his hands cupped her cheek. "I think they would say you have a dusting of freckles. This island sun brought them out. They were a lot darker when you were a girl."

Her blood began to hum through her veins at his touch. She leaned into his grasp like a cat wanting to be petted, but then drew back. "So I was a freckle-faced girl with red hair. Did I have the temper to match?"

"*Uh-huh*, especially when you didn't get your way. But you weren't bad for a squirt of a girl."

She flipped the sketchbook closed. "Any other details you care to share?"

"Nope." He carried his art supplies and two empty tea glasses back into the house. She sulked when he didn't come back immediately.

Standing by the door he asked, "How about a boat ride?" She jerked at his voice. "Sorry, I didn't mean to sneak up on you."

"I thought you needed to get back to work. I'm fine. You don't have to be the camp activities director on my behalf." When he said nothing, she turned to look at his face. "What?"

His missing eyebrow appeared to rise. Another thought crept into her mind. "Do I remember watching another birth with you? Was it kittens? We both were younger and the details faded. It was an old building cracking in the sun's heat." She could almost smell hay.

"Maybe, maybe not, I don't remember that. Maybe it was someone else you were with?"

"No, I think it was you, buster. Don't deny it, but a boat ride sounds nice. You said the engine was broken?"

"Before there were engines, there were sails and oars."

He gave her a hat he grabbed from his rack by the door and stepped down the stairs to the sand. She hesitated, and then grasped his uplifted hand. His warm firm clasp squeezed away any hesitation. After unlocking a shed door, Grayson pulled out an inflatable dinghy, pump, and oars. She watched as he stomped the accordion-like air pump. The pumped air lifted the rubber into shape; the sides filled out. He stacked the pump back inside the shed and pulled out life jackets and a bailer. He cracked open a flat of water bottles and tossed several into the boat.

She stood aside, holding her folded elbows in her palms. She turned to watch the dog and laughed. "Casey's barking as if he's saying 'Oh boy, oh boy. We're going for a boat ride.'" When she looked back, Grayson gave her a stern glare. "What now?"

"A little help would be nice." He assembled the craft and lifted up one side with the rubberized handle.

"Aye, aye, captain." She walked to the other side and lifted. "*Uh*! Not as light as it looks."

“We don’t have to carry it far. I want to get it over the dune and oyster rock before we set it down. You think you can do that?”

“Yeah, I’m getting my rhythm now. I’ll let you know if I need to stop. Is this the boat you go to town in?”

“No.”

“Well, don’t be so mysterious. Where is it?”

“I keep it in the back of that shed. During the summer, I keep it tied at my dock on the sound, where Ella comes in. I bring it in once the weather gets cold. All it does in the cold months is bang against the dock. I don’t go to town very often.”

“I see. More mysteries, like how did you get the big boat into your shed? Did you put the boat away so it wouldn’t look too available to me?” He ignored her line of questioning, which frustrated her more. When they came to the hard damp sand, Grayson stopped and shoved the raft into the shallow water. Lise climbed in and sat on the back seat. Casey waited for a command, his tail wagging like a banner.

“Get in and sit.” Grayson snapped his fingers. The dog jumped in past Lise, climbing forward into the round bow. Grayson walked them into deeper water and then eased his legs up and into the boat. He slid the oars into the oarlocks. “This will be your job.” He handed her a cut-off bleach bottle. “If the water gets past your ankles, I’d advise you to start bailing. We won’t sink but we’ll get very wet.”

"You get bossy on the water, Captain. Is this your way of telling me that I couldn't do all this by myself?" She felt the cool water seeping in over her feet.

"Are you thinking about trying to do this all by yourself?" His eyes narrowed.

"No, you proved your point." She scooped two jugs of water, tossing them over the side.

"You're doing that like an old salt."

"I'm supposed to be enjoying this ride, aren't I?"

"*Uh-huh*, smile. We're having fun." He flashed a grin and spun the rubber boat around masterfully.

She watched the shore as he rowed along the length of the island, but glanced back at him often. His muscles moved easily with every dip of the oars. Now she knew why his chest and arms looked so firm.

"It's too shallow along this part of the island to get here by boat unless you use a pontoon raft or flat-bottomed boat."

She looked over the side of the dinghy. The boat skimmed over the salt water flats. Occasionally, sea-grass floated by or a crab skittered in the boat's shadow. Minnows scattered out of their way. She also saw tracks on the shore from her earlier journey and the muddy place where her feet began to sink. As they progressed, she made a mental map of the shoreline.

"You're concentrating too hard. Your forehead looks plowed. Relax." He worked the oars easily as they glided over the water. She scooped to his rhythm. One scoop to his three pulls. Cumulous clouds climbed from the west. The sun streamed around the edges.

"Looks like a Thomas Kinkade painting." He touched her arm and pointed.

Lise turned as his warmth caressed her. She saw where the sun beamed down on a stand of trees. "Look. They have a new one, too." A tiny spotted colt danced along the water's edge, ignoring his mother's neigh. She tossed her head and trotted over, giving him a nip on his back. He returned to the safety of the herd, shaking his tail.

He watched the disappearing herd and said, "Children are a trial, even for four-legged mamas. But I suppose they are a blessing, also. Being part of a family is good."

"If I had children, I'd take them to the beach every day."

He nodded.

She continued to prod him. "I'm not married. I have no children. Right?"

"That part you need to remember yourself. I knew you a long time ago, remember." He smiled again, "I'm learning more about you each day you're here."

She liked his face when he smiled. It broke from his mouth, creasing his cheeks. Even his eyes twinkled beneath the brim of his hat. "Being on the water is something I know. Can we go fishing? I remembered I like to fish. My children will fish and love the water. This boat ride jogged my mind. I used to go sailing when I wanted to get away."

"Good. You're right about both the fishing and the sailing. Who or what were you trying to get away from back then and what or who were you escaping from last week?"

"When I was little, it was my family or Daddy. I don't think I liked the man very much. I can't imagine what I'm trying to get away from now."

"You did have an old boat. I think it was your uncle's."

"My uncle's?" His leg leaned into hers, reminding her of their physical closeness. She felt heat zap between their shins and liked the feeling of his nearness. Was she feeling attracted to him? Even he admitted he was unsightly, but as she studied his face, she disagreed.

"You aren't really ugly, just different looking." As soon as she said it, she knew she had erred.

He stopped rowing and asked, "What brought that on?"

"Don't get upset. I'm telling you something you should know. I'm comparing you to other men I know. I mean, in my mind, I see flashes of men dressed in business suits, ties, and long-sleeved shirts with cuffs barely showing at their wrists." She pretended to pull a cuff down on her wrist. "Their haircuts styled somewhere besides a corner barbershop, moussed and flicked for flair." Again, she used her fingers to pull imaginary hair around her head. She had smoothed over her comment about him with her chatter. "You have a nice face, even without the hair."

"Again, I wouldn't know. I'm thinking of always keeping mine shaved." No emotion showed on his face as he stared back.

Grayson's face was becoming attractive to her. She stared at his head trying to imagine it with hair -- and more smiles.

Again, the vertigo swirled her vision. "Whoa, I think I'm getting seasick. Is that possible?" She grabbed the sides of the boat waiting for the nausea to pass.

"Are you sure looking at me didn't make you sick?" He frowned.

"No! Why do you say those things?'

He nodded towards the sound. "Look out at the horizon, away from the boat. That should help your stomach. Don't watch me up close." There was concern in his eyes.

She focused her gaze up and away from his. The ponies were moving away from the shore. "Are they all wild? Who owns them?"

"Some have brands. The owners come over every year to mark the new ones or take them off. The management is questionable. If there's too many, they die. Mine are free, but they come back. I'm a pushover when they come to the fence and nicker for dinner." He stopped rowing and the wind carried them back a ways. "I enjoy their company. They'll drift away later this spring and return in the fall when the grass gets sparse.

"I'd hate to see them go."

"I do." He stirred one oar in the water, turning the dinghy around and let it blow back in the direction of the house. "My job gets easier now, but you still have yours." His toe tapped hers as water rose around their bare feet. Using one oar, he guided the boat, powered by wind and current, back along the shoreline. "It's about two miles to the next island depending on the tide and if we have any bad storms. This used to be one long strand, but a hurricane forged the inlet years ago, dicing us up like carrots on a cutting board. The higher end of the island with the forest of tropical palms and oaks over there was sliced from my section. I have a few stands of trees here and lots of sand. At the inlet between us, the current can get very rough. At this time of the year, when we have really low tides, you can walk between them." His gaze caught hers. "I only travel off island when the wind and current are agreeable. Even with the outboard, it's tricky.

"I get the message. No escaping this island without your assistance." She blew a long exaggerated breath and looked down. "I'd like to escape my nightmares, not your island."

While his hands felt the oars, his eyes watched her fidget in her seat. He thought back, silently remembering her from years ago. Her child smell, his grabbing her ponytail, the way she connived for his attention. Grayson relished her comment about not wanting to leave his island.

He didn't want her to leave, well, at least not until she remembered. He watched her eyes narrow. She licked her lips. That tiny pink tongue whipped out to wet her lips, once more. He was fascinated with the way her lips and tongue moved over one another, until it hit him. It wasn't a sensual penchant, she needed water, damn it! He grabbed the bottles of water.

"Here, drink this. I don't want you dehydrated."

Taking the bottle, she cracked the seal and drank half the water without stopping. After he drank from his water bottle, he poured some in his hat for the dog to lap. When Casey drank all the wetness from the make-shift cup, she added the rest of her bottle.

"You didn't have to share, but thanks. You both looked thirsty. He was panting."

The dog circled and sat in the water between them, pushing their legs closer together.

Grayson didn't mind the feel of her legs against his own. Their bodies balanced in the special way two magnets hover apart from one another and turn as their poles reverse. He needed to get back to work before he started comparing themselves to something other than cold hard metal. "I have two more paintings to finish before my show next month. I'll find you some books or you can paint if you'd like." He wondered if she'd try.

"I don't think I can paint anything more than my nails." She held them up for his approval.

"Do what you want. I need to get back to work this evening." He turned the boat toward shore. It bounced in the ripples as they landed. She bent to roll her wet cuffs up once she was on dry sand. He noted how the new pants hugged her hips. Men appreciate different parts of a woman's body and he knew he was definitely a "hip" man. She turned into him, bumping his chest. On impulse, he grabbed her arms and pulled her close. His mouth closed over hers. Her lips were dry, but forgiving. His hands grabbed her hair and pulled her lips into his for one long, heated kiss. He felt as if he could inhale all of her in one greedy gulp. Her breasts pushed into his chest and her feet brushed cold wet sand against his.

She seemed to want more. Her hands were on his neck and reaching up. "No, don't. Don't touch my head. I hate….' He stepped back. "I'm sorry." He remembered the feel of her fingers briefly kneading his neck and climbing up to tip his hat aside. "I shouldn't have done that. I couldn't help myself. I had to taste you…. "

He cleared his throat. "Well, no more manhandling the castaway. I promise I'll control all future urges." She was smiling at him like a woman smiles at a man. "No really, I'm old enough to be your, well, at the least your older brother." He couldn't help himself, so he added, "Or your teacher even."

"Were you?" She grinned and reached down in the water to spray a handful of water at him. "Were you my high school art teacher? It's all right, you know. I kissed you back, ole man." She straightened her pullover shirt and smoothed her slacks.

He said nothing.

"*Ahem*, as you were, Captain. Crew awaits further orders." She gave him a smart salute. He nodded and together they lifted the dinghy and carried it back to the house.

NINE

He pulled a newspaper-wrapped package from the bottom drawer of his refrigerator. “I hope you like fish.” He chose a favorite knife and took the fish outside to gut and scale it. Returning, he tore off an arm’s-length of tinfoil from the roll. He placed the striped fish on the foil, sprinkled it with oil, sliced potatoes, bacon strips and tucked garlic around the edges. Sealing the whole thing into an envelope of sorts, he placed it into the oven. “Late lunch ok as an early dinner?”

“Sure. I like only having two meals a day. What can I do?” She washed her hands. “I can make us a salad.”

“Sounds good.” He gathered dishes and set the table.

She opened the door to the refrigerator, sorting through the vegetable bin. “Tomatoes, carrots, celery, lettuce, olives and goat cheese. You have a well-stocked garden here, Captain. I can make a meal on all this. Yes,” she stopped. “I like Greek salads and olives. I remember a big kitchen with pots and pans hanging from the ceiling rack -- an island in front of the stove top, marble counters, stainless steel appliances and at the window, an herb garden. Am I right?” In her mind, she felt the cool surfaces and smelled a woodsy fireplace flavor in the room.

"How do you feel about that?" He stood aside watching her.

"Good, but there's something sad about it all." She frowned as she opened the container of olives and changed the subject. "I love olives. Lucky, for you." She gave him one and popped another in her mouth. Grayson raised his eyebrows. The invisible eyebrows were getting more active in her mind. She thought about the kiss and the way his body felt against her. She enjoyed both his kiss and the embrace. His lips were cool and inviting. She wanted more. She knew she wanted more.

Lise slammed the wide blade of the chef's knife against the garlic clove and minced it into a fine meal as she mixed the salad dressing. "*Huh*, I know this recipe by heart. I didn't even have to think about it." With one eye, she watched him.

"You are simply amazing. Are you sure you aren't a talented chef?" He teased her with the generous compliment. "Not everyone knows how to squash a garlic clove or make a decent salad dressing."

"Thank you, monsieur." She bowed graciously. "That fish was a sheephead, good eating. Did you catch it?"

"No, Ella thought you'd like it."

"*Uh huh.* She's another mystery for me." She pushed out both of her lips in a pout. "Do I know her, too?" She tossed the carrots over the top of the salad. "Is that why you won't let me talk with her?"

He didn't respond.

"Here's an easy question you can answer. How does the refrigerator work?" She went over to the refrigerator door and pulled it open to replace the unused vegetables.

"When it needs power, it kicks on the generator outside. A lot of islanders have them rigged that way."

"Not so hard to answer that one, was it?" She followed him into the other room.

While dinner cooked, he lined all his paintings along the walls of the small living room. "I need something else here and more light here. What do you think?"

"If your paintings sell, you're the better judge." In spite of herself, she studied each painting. "That one needs something."

"Definitely." He placed the picture of a beach cottage on his easel and thought about what to do.

Lise pulled a book from a stack on the end table. It was a discarded John Updike library book. The end pages were library stamped "Southport" and the cardholder torn from the back cover. She noted several of the books were in worse shape. "Are we close to Southport?" She held the book up so he could read the stamp.

"Yes."

"So you buy your reading material from the library book sales. I've gone to a few."

"Lise, I'm trying to paint for one undisturbed hour. Is that too much to ask?"

"Sorry, again." She noticed certain pages turned down throughout the book and decided to read those pages satisfying her idle curiosity. Updike's Rabbit was having problems and sexual dilemmas again. Someone had noted every mention of sex in the volume by bending the corner of the page down. She grinned wondering if it was a lonely librarian. Surely, it wasn't Grayson or his deceased wife.

Lise watched Grayson as he stood with a finger tucked between his lips, chin on his thumb, and one elbow supporting the other. A gentle shiver crawled around the back of her head in a pleasing sort of way. He'd changed hats again, now wearing a fishing cap with hooks tucked in the sides. He moved about adding dots of color. Casey snored softly, slumped against the wall.

A timer rang calling them to the meal. She stood and stretched, feeling like part of a couple. He dumped his brushes in the ever-present brush cleaner jar and she noted the page number of her book. They walked into the kitchen. She dipped wooden tongs into her bowl of greens while he carefully opened the fish package.

"*Hmm*, smells wonderful," Lise said. "You don't happen to have a bottle of wine tucked away somewhere do you?

"No, I don't drink alcohol." His sharp response even startled the dog.

She feigned disdain. "Maybe I'd like a glass, if you don't. I remember liking a glass of wine with a meal."

"Sorry, no wine and no booze of any kind." He spoke low, like ice crunching under tires. "Want to hear about my year with a bottle?" Again, his invisible eyebrow jerked.

Lise shook her head. "Not especially."

"I'm a recovering alcoholic, Lise, another strike against me." He poured her a glass of sweet tea. "That's why you won't find wine or beer here. When a drunk killed my wife, I started drinking. Ironic isn't it? It took me a year to realize she wasn't coming back and I needed to get on with my life." He tore open the foiled fish and potatoes. "I'm not asking for pity. I want you to know why I don't drink." He shoveled out the meal onto their plates.

"Well, foods a'waiting. Shall we?" She forked a large portion of salad on the plates. Provoked by his comments, she chided him, "Poor man, you're a recovering cancer patient, alcoholic, grouch and hermit! Here I've come and destroyed your peace and quiet. I wonder if you have any other vices?" She bit her tongue. *Why can't I keep my big mouth shut?*

"So we are going to discuss our vices. You, my dear woman, are rude, nosey and always in a constant flurry with that Type-A personality of yours." He shoveled food into his mouth. "You are pestering, bossy and, and…."

"Forgetful?" She gave him her best Cheshire cat imitation. "You left out that one. Can you think of anything else? Too bad. Now you've ruined my appetite." She stood, mumbling, "The fish wasn't half bad."

"What's that?"

Turning Lise said, "Your fish was good. I liked it. End of today's compliments."

"Don't leave in a huff. I'm sorry that we said all that. Sit back down and finish your meal. I don't want you going home and saying I didn't feed you here."

"Oh, so you are going to let me go home?" She sat back down and popped another olive in her mouth.

"I said when you remembered a few important things, you could go."

"If you tell me what is so important, maybe I'll remember it." He shook his head. They finished their meal in silence. "If you're through, I'll do the dishes and you can do whatever you did before I came." She flipped the hand towel in a snap. He went outside for a while and returned to his paintings. "You wash tomorrow and I'll feed the critters." With that, she took her book upstairs to read.

***

Grayson prowled the downstairs looking through his canvasses after she left. He lit the trio of thick candles on the mantel, lowered and lit the ceiling-hung kerosene lantern. It still wasn't light enough to suit him, but perhaps nothing could satisfy that evening. Grayson regretted his outburst. His timing was out of kilter. He needed to get started earlier in the day. Lise was destroying his rhythm. Their kiss and then their fight continued to nag at him. He'd ruined everything with his kiss and then his admission about the drinking. It was stupid of him to open up to her. Perhaps he should stick with his mad painter image and not acknowledge any interest in her. He didn't have the time to court her anyway. She'd be gone by the end of the week if she remembered it all.

Close to midnight, he wiped his brushes clean on a rag and climbed the stairs. He wondered for the hundredth time if he should tell her about her brother. If Ted hadn't died, would she have come back? His hand kneaded the back of his neck. Grayson showered by moonlight, pulled on gym shorts and promptly fell asleep on his side of the bed.

TEN

As the back door clicked shut the next morning, Grayson's eyelids popped opened. She'd awakened earlier, dressed quietly, and crept down the steps. "Confound that woman!" The dog jumped at his voice. Grayson stalked to the door of his deck to see what path she took. "Casey, go with her." He scrambled down the steps and threw open the screen door. The dog circled, skittering across the floor, and then raced out of the yard.

Satisfied, Grayson returned upstairs to dress. His fingertips roamed his face and head carefully. There were places where the hair was coming back in patches. He wondered how bad it looked as his fingers searched for more evidence of growth. Months of going without hair meant his morning toilet took less time for shaving or combing his hair. "Maybe I'll take the wait-and-see approach on this."

His bacon-frying stopped when Lise said she didn't like it. With her out of the house, he pulled a package from the refrigerator. While the large black skillet heated on the stove top, he made a pot of coffee and assumed his pre-Lise mode. Before he perched at his seat, he pulled another Updike book from the stack of books. Grayson read eating his bacon, toast and eggs. Afterwards, he fed the animals and gathered fresh eggs. He headed in the opposite direction for his walk. Without Lise around, he'd paint more. Annie was Lise. She no longer carried the implications of Annie's family and their past together. And the name, Grayson, appealed to him as well. Was it because she gave it to him? His mind kept drifting back to her.

***

The cloudless sky domed the island as far as Lise could see. She took a deep breath and then ran to the ocean. She gasped as the cold water covered her feet, but soon grew used to it and kicked sea foam in the air. *I don't need him looking after me. Who does he think he is anyway? All I have to do is remember who I am and I can go home.*

Lise smiled at Casey's bark. She stooped to catch the dog in a morning hug. "*Hmm*, so the Master sent you after me, *eh*? Well, we can enjoy the day without his lording over us." She sat in the dry sand and shared her breakfast sandwich and water with the dog. With breakfast behind her, Lise headed to the northern end of the island.

A cool wind chopped up the ocean as Casey chased birds along the shore. She pulled the plaid shirt closer; glad she's picked it up when she left. She could smell him in the shirt so it wasn't totally escaping the man. Lise took deep breaths as she walked, trying to fill the void in her head, urging memories to float up. The tide was low allowing them to wade across a wide flat where the ocean and sound met. A flounder kicked up sand in the water as it skated to a new bed.

The dimpled sand shifted each time she placed her foot down. The pull of the water on her thighs reminded her of the cross-country ski machine she used for morning workouts. *I see my whole gym. There are stair climbing and rowing machines also. My walls are pale green and skylights filter the light. There's a flower garden outside the French doors.* As beads of sweat formed on her face, her thighs plowed harder through the water. She remembered her home or at least part of it. *Mama and I breakfast together every morning. How about that?* She saw an older African-American woman bringing in a pitcher of juice. *Zerada!* Relieved by the newly surfaced memories, she waited impatiently for more pictures of her former life.

The dog chased crabs and minnows zigzagged in the shallows. Sea grass gave way to fine shells and hard packed sandy beach. Scrubby oaks trimmed low by the wind hugged the shore. Cedars and myrtles thickened along her path. Birds flitted in the woods, chirping out warnings as she approached. The dog found a path and Lise followed, as insects buzzed her head.

Hornets, swarming above her head, stopped her. She crouched holding her knees as panic replaced her confidence. She remembered when she was five, being trapped above her grandmother's hen house where she went exploring one hot summer day. She had climbed the banister-free steps to the top of the building without telling anyone. Her grandmother was busy and her mother didn't care what she did. The heat cracked the ancient walls and the tin roof popped. Her skin and clothes were smeared with sweat and the red clay dust she'd raised during her exploration. A disintegrating cardboard box hugged a half dozen Mason jars and lids. Her prowling uncovered a pitchfork with only three tines, old curtain drying racks, and a pickle crock.

She turned to leave, but the child, Lise, discovered the open door through which she had crept was the home of a large hornet nest bulging out from the top of the doorframe. The insects swarmed around their home. Frightened, Lise screamed for help, but no one came. It seemed like hours when someone finally showed up. Her face was red from crying. Damp hair clung to her head. She gasped for breath when her brother found her. Her clothes were damp from her young sweat and tears. She trembled at his touch. Hiccupping, she clung to his neck.

"It's alright, Peanut. See, those old hornets could care less about us. Hold my hand and we'll get you outside." Teddy had found her, hugged her and helped her escape. Teddy was her hero.

Lise remembered her big brother's name. She looked down, listening to the flying insects as they drew her back to the present. He called her Peanut. For the time being, she preferred Lise. She swished gnats away with a branch she broke off a myrtle tree. She stood and walked further along the path. A pond, complete with a rocky landscaped edge, cattails and lily pads appeared. The frogs quieted as she neared, but soon the croaking and chirping of creatures began again.

Casey returned, sniffed at her legs and continued back on his path.

Underfoot, the ground softened. She carefully picked her way through the low limbs of water oaks and loblolly bays. Casey hesitated and then jumped through a thick bank of undergrowth. “Hey, stop. Don’t leave me. Where did you go?” A one-story white bungalow with a row of windows across the back hunkered between the trees. Built in an island plantation style with red tin roof, shutters, and a wide wrap-around porch, it nestled among oleanders, myrtles and gardenia bushes. Lise walked around hanging ferns and a porch swing to the front door.

Casey padded up to the door and drank from a water dish before slumping on the porch. “Have you been here before or are you mooching from someone else’s bowl?” She knocked on the silent door. No one answered. She knocked again, and then peered through the window. A wide entry led into other rooms. Covered furniture, like ghosts in a bad play, stooped across the floor. “*Hmm*, another mystery.” She walked along the porch peeking in windows as she came to them. In the dimness, she made out an open floor plan, interior columns and fireplace.

Pine straw covered the flowerbeds. Spikes of daffodils and irises were breaking through the cover. She peered into an outbuilding and saw all-terrain vehicles and jet skis stacked on a utility trailer. She followed a driveway down through the trees to a landing and wide docking area. Marsh odors tickled her nose with saltiness. In the distance, she saw another island or was that the mainland? *Why didn't Grayson mention the house?*

Her stomach growled. She had left the house around six and walked almost four hours. A gray heron took flight, screeching and Lise remembered being here before. She reached out to grab a piling as a shadow crossed her mind. Someone pushed and knocked her down in this same spot. Her skin cooled to a numbing chill and her stomach lurched. She threw up in the water. She heaved several times more before her stomach settled. Casey stood at her side and whined. Exhausted from retching, Lise crumbled to her knees, head down and waited. It felt better to lie on her back. She took slow breaths regaining control of her stomach. The dog slumped down beside her.

The last thing she remembered was the cloudless blue sky overhead.

***

"Miss, missy. Are you alright?" A hand touched her arm and shook her awake. Lise looked into faded blue eyes and a wrinkled face, shadowed by a wide brimmed hat.

The crone coughed into her shoulder. "Taking a little nap were you? I seen you here when I was going by. You staying with Mr. Armstrong, are you? I was jest going that way. You and the dog want a lift back, honey?" The woman pulled a pack of Camels from the pocket of her shirt and lit one. She picked a bit of tobacco from her tongue and flicked it into the water. "I don't s'pose you want one of these?" She offered the pack.

It took a few seconds for Lise to regain her composure. She shook her head carefully. “No thank you. I don’t smoke.”

“A good thing, too. It’s a nasty habit once’t you start.” She blew a long stream of smoke away from Lise.

“Are you Ella? Grayson told me about you.”

“Don’t know no Grayson. I bring Mr. Armstrong out things he wonts and leave h’m be.” She spoke with the island brogue.

“Yes. Please, take me home? I mean, I want to get off these islands.”

“Oh, no, missy, can’t do that. They look’n for you the’yar. You don’t want t’be going t’the mainland. You safe where y’are, here.” She patted Lise’s arm as she talked.

“Who’s looking for me? Why is it safer here?”

Motionless the woman stared back at her.

“Can you tell me my real name, then?”

“No, again you’ll have to ask Mr. Armstrong. I’ll take you back to him. Come aboard, Casey.” She gave a sharp whistle and the dog hopped down into the skiff.

Layers of white paint plastered the seat and sides of the wooden skiff. Nets, floats and other fishing gear lay in the floor. A bucket of fresh caught fish stood in the shade of the seat.

“Did you catch that sheephead we ate last night?”

“Yep.” For the first time, the woman smiled a tobacco-stained greeting. “You liked it then? He cook it with potatoes and bacon?”

Lise nodded.

"He's a good cook when he sets his mind to it." The older woman watched her charges as she backed away from the dock and rounded the island. The wooden boat had a wide flare bow that cut through the waves. The in-board engine provided a covered resting place for Ella's arm. She drew another deep breath on her cigarette. Lise noted her stained chipped fingernails, the faded tee shirt and elastic waist jeans. After her final drag, the woman flipped the butt away. She coughed several times more and cleared her throat. "I'm damned if I do and dammed if I don't smoke, 'scuse me. Em-pho-sema."

"You shouldn't be out here like this." Lise showed her concern by reaching over and grabbing Ella's hand.

Ella barked a deep cough, shaking her head, then tapped the motor cover to draw the attention away from her illness. "What'd you say honey? I can't hear very good. Y'ever been on a tunnel drive boat? Noisy, but we can get through thin water. Yes-siree, Bob. She's a thin water boat."

Lise nodded she understood then turned back in her seat.

Ella steered from the back corner while Lise faced front on the opposite side holding the dog's head. The breeze blew her hair away from her face. She had no idea how long she slept. The sun was high in the sky.

"What time is it? Can you tell me?" She looked back, tapping her wrist.

"Oh, it's about 2-3 o'clock, afternoon for sure. I don't wear a watch. At my age everything is now." Ella cackled in the wind.

They passed the inlet between the islands now covered by the rushing tide. Lise recognized the beach and shoreline.

"Mr. Armstrong's waiting for us. See." The older woman pointed with her chin.

"Could I ask you a favor before we get there? Can we keep a secret? Will you get me a pregnancy test at the store? I don't want him to know. Will you do that?" She watched Ella consider the request.

Finally, the older woman pushed out her bottom lip and chin. She nodded. "I'll do it and I sneak it in a package of undies. How's that?" Lise thanked the woman as they neared the shore. Ella slowed the boat, cutting the engine. The boat drifted in, running aground in the soft sand.

"I see you've met." Grayson held the boat as Lise climbed out. "Did Ella tell you her father built this boat? It's a traditional Harker's Island skiff. I've painted it in a couple of my pictures."

"No, she didn't. But she did tell me some interesting things. Ella, thank you." Lise walked past Grayson away from the shore.

He shrugged, replaced his canvas bag of recyclables for the one of supplies she brought and thanked the elderly woman. "You have enough money? "

She coughed as she nodded and pointed at Lise. “She’s a handful ain’t she?” When Grayson nodded back, a brief smile on his face, she cackled again. “She grow’d up a looker. She’ll do real fine.” She winked and then pulled away from the island.

Grayson followed Lise to the house.

“Why does she call you Mr. Armstrong? She’s old enough to be your mother.”

He jerked around. “What makes you say that?”

She shrugged.

“You’ll have to ask her then.”

Lise looked in the refrigerator when they arrived. She took a jar of jam, “Do you have crackers?” She bent over the sink and splashed water on her sunburned face.

He pulled a towel from a drawer and handed it to her. “They’re in the breadbox.” She pulled a knife from another drawer and sat at the table making tiny jam and peanut butter sandwiches with the round crackers, stacking them together.

He unpacked cans and packages from his canvas bag, not certain of her mood. Grayson handed her a pair of web-strapped sandals. “Do you like these?” He slapped them on the table by her castle turrets of crackers.

She looked at the tag. “Not my style, but they’ll do.” She cut off the tags and Velcro’d the strap across her foot. She held them up for his approval. “You like?”

“Nice.” He hid his interest, admiring not only the foot, but also the ankle, calf and long leg that disappeared into her shorts. "What kind of shoe would you wear?" He gave her another one of his quick tight-lipped smiles.

"Something strappy, with little heels, I think. Ella said they're looking for me ashore. Did you know?" She raised her gaze from her upturned foot to his eyes. "She wouldn't take me over. You told her not to. So full of mysteries you are. What about that beautiful house at the end of the island -- who lives there?"

"You went all the way there?"

She nodded her mouth now full of crackers.

"Here, look. She got you some nail polish. I hope you like the color. There's no remover in the sack." He chewed on his lip while he thought. "She said they were looking for you. Anything else?"

She shook her head, hair brushing her shoulders.

"If I *lost* you, I'd look for you. Now, if you *ran away* from me, well that's a different story."

"Would you now?" She took the empty bags and hung them by the door in their usual place as she waited for more answers.

"The house is empty. They never come anymore. A caretaking service comes over once a month. Not much more to tell." Her brother, Ted Basnight, had finagled a land sale buying the nearby island. The land had belonged to Grayson's grandparents who forgot to pay taxes during their final years. Ted had bullied the county tax office into selling it to him for back taxes before Grayson could do anything about it. Ted Basnight had owned the lush tropical forest island. Grayson owned the sparsely covered scrub pine and cedar grove end of the stretch. Grayson's stomach tightened every time he thought about the two strips of land.

"Grayson, or should I say Mr. Armstrong, you specifically told her not to give me a ride across the sound?" Lise chewed the crackers slowly, concentrating on making another tower of cracker-jam sandwiches and eating her way through them.

"Yeah, I did."

She got up, poured herself a glass of milk and sat back down. "I see. I don't understand, but I see. Shall I call you Mr. Armstrong from now on?"

"No, Grayson is the name you gave me. I'm getting used to it." He refilled Casey's water bowl and went back to his painting.

She followed him, taking the nail polish. "I remembered something else." Taking off her new sandals, she shook the bottle and bent over her feet. "Whoa, I still get dizzy when I lean down." She looked up. "What is it with me and this spinning?"

"Give me that. I'm the painter, remember?" Grayson pulled a chair from the kitchen and lifted her foot into his lap. He studied her toes for a minute then gruffly repositioned her foot. He dabbed the brush into the thick polish and painted a large toenail. "Golly. This is tougher than it looks." He swallowed a laugh. "How often do you have these polished?"

"Are you laughing at me, Mr. Armstrong? It's been my experience that you didn't know how to laugh." She teased him. "I think if I were the type of girl - who had painted my toenails, I'd have them done every month." She wiggled her toes in his face.

"Stop that. Be still. I can laugh if something's funny." His hand wavered holding the tiny brush. She jerked every time he touched a nail. "Quit moving." He shook her foot.

"I can't help it. My foot thinks you're tickling me."

"Are you ticklish? I need something in my arsenal to make you behave." He frowned and then laid the small lid-brush on a rag and reached for one of his own long handled paint brushes.

She grimaced, trying to keep her foot still and balanced between his legs. "They want to curl up when you touch them. They have a mind of their own. I'm sorry. I've never had a man paint my toenails before."

"So I'm your first."

"What are you suggesting, Mr. Armstrong? Not to worry," she made her point by fluttering her hand across her breast, "you wouldn't be my first." Lise smiled sweetly knowing exactly where she was leading him.

He cleared his throat and re-applied another coat. "Talk about something else. It's to keep your mind off what I'm doing. You said you remembered something." He put the first foot down and lifted the other. Lise leaned her head back on the couch and tried not to watch him.

"Oh, yes. I remembered visiting my grandmother's hen house one summer day. My granny had chickens like yours, the speckled ones"

Grayson continued carefully filling in every bit of nail with polish, dabbing the brush each time he started a new nail.

"There was a big hornet nest. It was hanging in the doorway. I never saw it when I went inside the loft. I must have been about five-years old. When I finished playing up there, I was too scared to leave. They were buzzing all around me. I squirmed into the back of the room to get away from them. Well, I screamed for help, but no one came. It was hot and I was filthy with nose-snot and crying. I was a mess, all sweaty and covered in tears and red dirt. Teddy, my brother, rescued me. He hugged me until I quit sobbing and called me Peanut. How's that for a recollection?"

Grayson forced a smile on his face as he handed her back the polish. "Do you approve of the finished product?" He felt like she'd punched him in the stomach. He stood up. "I need to get back to my real painting, if you'll excuse me." He returned the kitchen chair and picked up the lacquered brush, wiping it on his cloth rag. "Nice story."

She remembered the hornet nest, but it was him -- not Teddy, who rescued her. Her young body convulsed in shudders and tears when he held her. Teddy found Grayson clutching the girl in his arms. Her brother humiliated her, calling her names for being afraid. That day was the last time

Grayson ever saw the girl cry. He wanted to break Teddy's neck.

ELEVEN

Lise fanned her toenails with her hand and then returned to the kitchen. She finished her snack as she listened to Grayson putter around his easel. She pushed back her chair and cleaned up her late lunch crumbs. Taking a towel from the counter, she fanned her newly painted toes until they were dry. The muscles in the back of her thighs ached from her morning walk as she climbed the stairs. A stack of tee-shirts, clean jeans and a small belt lay on her side of the bed. *Has he washed clothes?*

She went to the top of the stairs. “Thanks for the clean clothes.”

She went down the steps, but he didn’t turn to acknowledge her. Lise found an abandoned milk carton crate on the back porch. She wiped it clean and carried it upstairs. After placing her clothes inside, she placed the box like an end table by her side of the bed. Pulling off the sheets and pillow cases, she grabbed the towels from the bathroom and went back downstairs. With her arms around the laundry, she leaned against the back door. “Show me how to work that antique washer and I’ll begin to earn my keep.”

She grinned at him the whole time he carefully explained how to work the old washer.

“If you overload it, it will waltz right off the porch.” Grayson instructed after showing her how to hook up the water hoses and use the rollers. “Remember, it’s rainwater. You don’t need a lot of soap. Any questions?”

“I think I’ve got it. Go do your painting thing, sir, and leave me to this.” She pulled the door open for him to retreat.

After the first load was through the ringers, she got into the rhythm of the machine. She washed, rinsed and used the rollers to squeeze out the excess water and then hung her first sheet on the clothesline. She propped her feet up on the porch railing and admired her painted nails as she flipped through the rest of Rabbit’s adventures. The old wringer washer’s tub took the linens in small gulps. When she had wrung out the third load, she was comfortable with the antique washer.

The first load of sheets was dry by the time she hung the towels beside them. She dropped the clothespin bag in the clothesbasket on the porch and sat watching the clouds cross their island until evening. Lise went out and then gathered them all in and folded them on the back porch. The mosquitoes found her and drove her inside.

“Is there enough hot water left for me to take a bath?” The smell of the oil paints and turpentine filtered throughout the little house as she climbed the stairs. She buried her nose in the sun-dried linens, inhaling as she climbed.

He pulled off his reading glasses and followed her to the bottom of the stairs. “There should be plenty. You washed with cold, didn’t you?”

“Yes.” She glanced back. “Are you watching my butt?”

He answered too swiftly, “Nope, never thought about it. Remember I promised no more attacking the castaway.”

“I can feel you eyes on my derrière, good sir.” Lise turned to face him. “Go back to your painting. See, *I’m* being good, Mr. Armstrong.” She used a sharp Southern twang.

He grinned up at her and then replaced the Ben Franklin spectacles on his nose.

“I’ve done my woman of the house stuff and now I’m taking a long relaxing bath.” Knowing he returned to his painting, she stripped off her clothes and played with the tub knobs until she mixed the right temperature.

The tub was an old footed vintage, with cracked enamel spigots. Her long legs had little room to stretch out. She left the water running until it covered most of her body. Knees out of the water, she slid down until all that showed were her breasts and the pearl ring. She ran her hands over her stomach and upwards. Lise took the soap and made a thick lather coating her feet, legs and stomach. *Is there tenderness? UGH! My legs need shaving.*

She reached for his razor beside the tub and soaped her legs again. *This will probably give him something else to complain about.* Alternating between having her legs under water and her shoulders, she finally settled with her head resting in the crook of the tub. Adding more hot water only made it pour out of the overflow faster.

As she twirled the pearl on the navel ring, the memory of the piercing came back. *Teddy got away with everything. I hated following Daddy's rules. "Be prompt." I couldn't wear the clothes like my friends did at school. "Be home by such and such time. I won't have you going out with those people! Keep up your grades." It wasn't fair.* She remembered her stubbornness. *I had to be sneaky when I rebelled against Daddy.*

Visions of her home, the people who worked there and the gardens slid through her mind. Her mother stayed in bed through mid-morning, until her father left for the office. It was like watching a silent movie as her mind roamed the home, exposing forgotten memories.

I was angry because Daddy wouldn't let me go to a party. I charged on my father's charge account at Ivey's Department Store, the briefest bathing suit I dared to wear. I drove over near the airport to find a tattoo parlor and had my navel pieced. It hurt like hell. Then I rushed to the country club that same morning and slathered oil on my body collecting glares or admiration from the pool-side guests. "You are coming home this minute, young lady, and I don't ever want to hear of you wearing that suit again!" Someone must have called my father. Daddy didn't even notice the pierced navel.

I had climbed out of my bedroom window by lunchtime and drove my little T-Bird to Southport, five hours away. Then there was my friend, Minnow, the older neighborhood boy. Minnow! Grayson was Minnow. Ka-chink. Teddy gave him that name because of the bait shop.

Another piece of the puzzle slid into place. Lise grinned wickedly, now remembering her childhood crush on her brother's friend. Whenever they went somewhere, she'd follow. That summer of the navel piercing, he was back visiting his parents, no longer a boy. *He kept backing away from me. Such a stern look he'd given me and pushed me away when I tried to rub up against him.*

"Your daddy is not going to be happy knowing you're here, Peanut." Minnow turned his back on me and lifted more boxes off a truck. I stood in his way so that he had to walk around me.

"You know neither my Daddy nor my Mama gives a damn about me, Minnow. I'm all grown up now. I'm a woman. Can't you see that?"

She flaunted her near-naked body at him again with the new bikini and navel ring

"I know your Daddy would shoot me and burn down my mama's store if he knew I looked at you twice. Now go home and pick on someone closer to your own age." Then things faded again. She didn't remember driving home. She remembered the large family home in Southport but she still couldn't recall her name. The memories churned up her

teenage infatuation on Minnow, smearing her body all over his and heaven only knows what else.

Well, I'm not a little girl anymore, Minnow-Grayson-Mr. Armstrong. Lise fingered the pearl again. She waited until the water cooled, then pulled a towel from the rack. The lingering smell of outdoors on the towel aroused her as she rubbed the fresh towel over her body. Its coarseness excited her more.

A fine coat of sweat seeped from her pores as she rinsed out the tub. Lise brushed her hair forward as she leaned over. Her head full of seduction, her body primed by memories, she left the top buttons unbuttoned on his long-sleeved denim shirt and decided to forego pants entirely. She brushed her teeth and then glided back down the stairs.

Grayson mashed the paint tubes as he mixed different shades of rose and peach. Lise interrupted but inspired his painting. He felt not only satisfied with the day's work but also aroused thinking about Lise upstairs in his bathtub. His body warmed thinking of her. He brushed his fantasy aside and used the stiff bristles to outline a picket fence on the dunes covered with flowers. On his painting, gulls circled in the sky. What would he put in the sand? A shoe, no a dropped sandal. He didn't recall how much time had passed, but he smelled her before he heard her.

She looked over his shoulder. "I like it. It's more impressionistic, softer. I like it very much." She came around to his side and smiled brilliantly.

"I didn't hear you come down. Wow. What did I do to deserve this?"

"I remembered you, Minnow."

He gasped. "You remembered Minnow." He held his arms at his side as she stepped closer. What she wore left nothing for his imagination. "I'm trying very hard to maintain my composure, Lise. Have mercy." Her newly painted toes touched his. Her hair was damp at her temples and flipped differently. Her lips appeared darker, fuller as she leaned closer, a woman in heat.

"Do you know what you are doing to me? If I lean a tad, our bodies will touch. Are you testing my will power?" He clasped his hands behind his back to keep them from wandering. "Lise, I'm not Superman with extraordinary powers. I haven't the strength or the will to push you away."

Her hand pressed against his chest. A flash of sexual heat arced between them. "I can feel your heart beating, Minnow."

"It's no wonder. I feel a timpani drum inside my chest at the moment." He took a deep breath. "You remembered me as Minnow. Anything else you care to share?"

"I had a humongous crush on you as a little girl, Minnow. And now that I'm a grown woman, Grayson, I intend to push it to the next level. I plan on taking advantage of you."

"You do?"

"*Uh-huh.*"

"And if I resist?"

"You won't." Her eyebrow went up and she smiled like the Cheshire again.

"Probably not, no man could resist you like this." Grayson lifted her wrist. He kissed her palm. She purred. He turned her hand and kissed her knuckles and fingernails. "We need to spend some time painting these." Her body chemistry had turned his man's soap into an enchanting perfume. He had wanted her for the past two days, but denied it. Grayson closed his eyes as he allowed her heat, her scent to saturate his space. Surprised again when his body responded so strongly to her, he leaned forward, nibbled along her neck with his lips and teased her with his breath near her ear.

"You have the beginnings of an evening shadow, my good man." Her fingers grazed his chin. "There's a bit of a beard growth and would you believe that excites me more."

"You can become more aroused than this? Stay on my island until I grow back all my hair."

"Silly man, would I leave you like this? What is this tiny scar on your cheek?"

She grinned when he said, "I fell off my bicycle."

She wondered if the other scars on his head would heal as nicely. "Sort of a Harrison Ford scar, a very sexy man, by the way." She shivered as he sucked her mouth into his lips. He gave her one long absorbing kiss, better than their first. He nibbled then sucked her ear lob and neck. Her desire mounted as his hands roamed the curves of her body. Her fresh-from-the-bath aroma and the smell of his oil paints created a passionate elixir for her.

Grayson pulled her body into his own wrapping his arms around her. Lise's fingers explored his face tipped his hat into the floor, felt his neck, and his ears. She gasped as he touched all the right places. His lips were cool, but they heightened her hunger for his taste. She kneaded his body, greedy for more.

She met him tongue to tongue, tempting him, inhaling his taste. His hands pulled up on her hips, bringing her closer. They feasted at each other's passion, feeling each other's bodies until skin touched skin beneath raised shirts. Lise discovered a trail of sweat on his spine that went below his waistband. Her fingers explored further and followed his backbone as far as she could reach.

He stopped and spoke softly. "Say you want me."

"Since forever, with every nerve of my being, I have always wanted you." She touched his lips with a forefinger and began unbuttoning his shirt. He pulled it over his head to speed up things. The island's sun had tanned his body. Her gaze followed her fingers as they roamed his chest. She felt him shiver under her touch. Another healed scar she'd never noticed ran around his side.

Her brief look ended when he pulled off her shirt, running his hands around her breasts while she unzipped his pants and pushed them down over his hips. As he continued to caress her, he stepped out of them, pushing them away from his easel.

The pleasure of stroking, touching, exploring each other continued when he backed her onto the couch. Arms and legs wrapped together like breakfast twists. The couch too short to sleep on held them like a cupped hand.

He flipped her down and crouched over her as he kissed her stomach. Kneeling above her, he teased her with his tongue. His thumb twirled around her breasts and the ring before going lower. She writhed in delight. When her fingers roamed the top of his ears and head, he never flinched. Her body arched and opened for his.

He gasped, "Lise." Her passion increased as their bodies responded to one another, delighting in their union.

A deep rumble rose from her throat when she climaxed, "Grayson!"

They collapsed together, puddling in one another's arms. Regaining a second wind Grayson moved his fingers back over her curves. "Before midnight, my eyes and hands will know every inch of your body."

****

She dreamed of sand, sun and oil paints. He slept as if he were drugged. Somehow, they both managed to stay on the short couch. As evening cooled the sands outside, she roused and nudged him.

"Well, what do we do for dessert? I'm starving." Lise grabbed her shirt and ran up to the bathroom.

"You're always hungry." He rolled off the couch, pulled on his pants and then went into the kitchen. He opened doors and looked at his pantry. She watched him a moment after she returned from pulling on a pair of jeans and his denim shirt.

Did I regret doing the deed? I can't judge his reaction. God, it was wonderful, but I had better not scare him away. "That was a one time thing for us, right? You probably do it all the time. You said there were others."

"What!"

"Was that, like a purely sexual response? It meant nothing to you but sex between a man and a woman?"

"Is that a flippant remark aimed to disguise your affection for me?" He turned.

"You don't even know me. It was all lust. Entirely my fault, I - "

She watched his eye muscle raise the invisible brow. His jaws moved back and forth grinding his teeth. Lise said, "You asked permission. I gave you the go ahead. By the way, I only remembered you from one incident, when I was a teenager."

"Only one time?"

"Yeah, I was angry at Daddy. I ran away from home and found you. But I know I must have been infatuated forever. The feeling was too strong."

"Infatuated?" He ran a finger down her forehead to her nose and caressed her chin with his thumb.

She said, "I still don't know my name. I remember my parents, a beach house and a bigger house somewhere. All of that came to me in your bathtub. And, oh, I wanted you. I wanted you BAD. Soaking in the water and thinking about you made me horny." She gave him a toothy smile. "I'm humping the host to get over my horniness!"

"Very alliterative, I think I'll give you more bath time." He tugged her closer. "As for your diarrhea of the mouth, we'll have to investigate." He sucked her lips and stroked his tongue against hers. "I hope it wasn't a one time thing." He continued to run his hands up her back under her shirt. "But if that's all you wanted…" He turned away from her and slammed the door to a cabinet. She jumped.

"Although it's a popular belief that all men will climb into the pants of any woman, I beg to differ. I admit I have thought about getting into your pants. Or shall I say my pants on you, a few times recently. Oh, what the hell." A navy Greek captain's hat was planted on his head. His cutoff denims hugged his hips. "Come here."

"You do look very jaunty. Is that a new hat?" She stepped towards him on the sandy floor. His fingers hooked into the belt loops of her jeans. He positioned her arms around his waist and pulled her close. His lips caressed her face. He kissed her twice more. "If I'm to be the humping host, I aim to please. Any further requests?"

"Nice, I like the attention." She patted his shoulder. "What you got to eat around here? I'm still hungry for food." At his moan, she nibbled his bottom lip.

He turned to forage in the pantry once more. "You like chocolate chip cookies?"

"As a matter of fact I do! What a clever man you are." She grabbed the bag of chocolate morsels, pulled out milk and eggs from the refrigerator. "Want me to feed the children tonight or cook? It is past their bedtime."

"I'll cook." He turned on the oven as she went out the door. "We'll all have a midnight snack." He lit the lantern and hung it on the outside hook.

Casey followed her out into the night. After she fed the horses and chickens, she found a tennis ball and threw it for the dog. The dog jumped and returned it every time until the smell of cookies drew them to the porch.

"Chocolate milk or plain," he asked.

"You have chocolate milk? It's one of my favorite-est things."

He turned to look at her as she peered through the screened door. She stepped inside the kitchen as he lumped two heaping spoons of cocoa powder into their glasses and stirred. "You wanted food. I've provided it." She stacked cookies on a plate and carried them out to the porch. He followed with the two glasses. "Comfortable?"

She propped her feet up on the porch railing and wiggled her toes. "Yes. Very nice. You never painted my toes before today, have you?"

"Today was my first-ever toe painting. No other woman in the world has had her toes painted by me. Shall I sign them for you?"

"Have we done this before?"

"The lovemaking, you mean?'

"*Uh-huh*."

"Do you remember doing this before?"

"Grayson, I'm serious. Are we lovers?"

"Would you like to be?"

"Answer me. No games, I want to know."

He put a whole cookie in his mouth; the chocolate smeared on his lips. "I don't remember us doing anything like what we just did, ever before." He proceeded to lick the melted chocolate from his fingers.

"You liked the sex." She watched as he sucked the melted chocolate from his lips. "It's frustrating when you don't give me whole answers."

He swallowed the cookie, took a sip of milk and said, "Would you have believed me if I told you, we were lovers the day you first saw me?" A long pause later, he shook his head. "Your open-mouth silence answers my question."

"Don't be so sensitive."

"Sensitive? I'm not being *sensitive*?"

"Grayson, please don't get upset."

"One of us has to be. This was the shortest affair in history. The afterglow hasn't even had time to fade." He stood to carry the empty plate inside.

"You're acting like a child."

"Am not!" He took her empty glass and then said. "Host-humping is quite an experience. I do have to be grateful for that."

She could hear him tidying up the kitchen and then all was silent. She counted 100 stars in the sky before she followed him. *He's sulking. It's not my fault. That first day I was afraid of him. The newness of him, the gruffness and his scars were a shock. Anyone would have had the same reaction. The man definitely has problems. I'm not the one to blame.*

When she finally climbed to the top of the steps, his quiet breathing on the far side of the bed was his only response. She brushed her teeth and climbed onto her side, waiting for him to roll towards her. He never did.

TWELVE

The cereal box and bowl sat on the table when she came down the next morning. Grayson and the dog were gone. Lise finished her breakfast and went out to the dock on the sound thinking they'd gone to meet Ella. No one was there. She walked the water's edge until she came to the marsh and returned, but they still weren't home. She found her book and took some cookies out to the porch. As she nibbled at the cookies and sipped the milk, her stomach kicked back with a jolt. Standing up, she retched over the railing. Leaning over and holding her knees with her palms, she waited until the queasiness passed and blood returned to her head. Feeling better, she pulled the hose from the side of the house to wash away any trace of her nausea.

An intelligent woman, by now, should be able to figure this out. If I was not pregnant before, I could be now. Or maybe I have some terrible disease. Maybe I have cancer. She was deep in thought when they trotted down the sand dune beside the house. Lise shoved herself up from the porch steps.

"I'm sorry about my reaction and leaving you last night. I was a fool." Grayson's voice deepened, "I missed you."

"Did you? I've been right here."

"Yes." He looked down.

"Are we friends again? I'd like being more than friends. I didn't have a chance to apologize yet," Lise cleared her throat."

"Look, you have nothing to be sorry about."

"I was rude to my host."

"Oh." He brightened.

"From now on, we'll discuss our feelings. That will make us better friends and lovers?"

"Lovers, you said lovers?" He smiled. "You'll give me the benefit of a doubt. I'm glad to hear I still have a chance at being more than a friend or host."

Running her fingers back through her hair, she pulled it tightly up behind her head. "Now don't get prickly. I have a question for you. Would you want to bed me if I had no hair? What if I had breast cancer and no -" She nodded down to her breasts, "you know? If you'd never met me before, would you be attracted to me? Would you?"

"I would, but I shouldn't have walked away last night." He came around the porch railing and placed his hands over hers, holding her hair back. "I'd want to make love to you hairless, without those lovely long legs or your sweet butt, without breasts, that lovely pearl in your navel and," his head jerked back, "-- why do I smell vomit coming from your lovely mouth?"

Grayson's hands fell to his sides as he stepped around her. He led her into the kitchen and removing his Cubby cap, scratched his head. He went to the sink and filled a glass of water. He squeezed lemon juice into it.

"Rinse, swish." He twirled his finger as he handed her the glass. When she did as he directed, he took her in his arms once more and said, "Now where was I?"

"You lost your moment, buster. You were saying you'd jump my bones no matter what until you smelled my breath."

"Ah, yes. We'll have to do something about that recurring messiness." He pulled a handful of condoms from his jeans pocket. "See? If you have another after bath inclination again or anything close to it, I'm prepared."

"What? Do they grow on trees on this island?"

"It'll look strange, but I can arrange it."

"I'm going to go brush my teeth. Want to come?" She gave him a Snoopy eyebrow dance, bobbing her brows up and down. Her heart hummed as she climbed the stairs. "Stop looking at my butt. I can feel your eyes running over my buns."

"I'm not looking at your butt. It's that slender line of skin between your shorts and your top that intrigues me." He followed her up the steps. She closed the bathroom door in his face.

"You know," he knocked on the bathroom door, "most men would have sex any time, anywhere. Are you listening?" She spit the last time and gargled behind the door. "I don't want Pity Passion. A man has to make a stand somewhere. I'm going to wait until I get some real lust out of you. Is that all right?"

She opened the bathroom door as he turned to go back downstairs and tapped him on his shoulder. Wearing nothing but her pearl, she leered at him. "Lust, did you say you wanted to wait for lust?" She licked her lips. "Lust at your service."

"Damn, I'm good." He caressed her body as he pulled her over to the bed. He fell on top of her, wiggled a bit to line himself over her and kissed her. "What now?" Grayson pulled himself up on his elbow to admire her.

"Don't you have a painting to finish?'

"I'm getting inspired. Now hush while I rapture you." He couldn't tug off his shorts fast enough. "You bewitch me. You know that, don't you? Here goes the whole morning, I'm afraid."

"If we're on a schedule, I'll set a timer. Now what was that you were saying about Pity Passion?" She threw one leg over his and continued with a wicked laugh. "Come here, my pretty."

***

The dog woke them with a loud bark. Both heads moved a fraction.

Grayson lay on his stomach, one arm draped over her body. He felt her stomach growl. "Are there any cookies left?" He lifted his head.

"Wise A-, how far did you have to go to the drugstore for those?"

"Did you know they make deliveries for emergencies?" He grinned as he turned her around and spooned her body into his.

"Did they only bring one handful or what's the deal?

"Woman, I ordered a whole case, but we will use them sparingly. I do have paintings to finish. I don't know how all those old masters did it with nude women lying at their feet. Life must have been tough."

"But it kept that rosiness on their skin, don't you think?" She rolled in his arms, to run a finger over his hand. "I don't think the Grand Masters complained. You can bank on it."

She enjoyed his nuzzlings for a moment, but then she punched him aside to yank herself upright. "Bank! I work at a bank, don't I? I remember an office, papers, thick carpeting, phones ringing, an elevator and floor to ceiling drapery." She leaned on her elbow. "Am I right? Tell me it's my office."

His satisfied smile opened into a gasp of shock. "Sort of like a bank. I think they call it an investment firm. Maybe I liked you better when you didn't remember. These little jolts of memory are hard for me to keep up with."

"If anyone is going to complain about pops of memory, it's me. Tell me what happened." She tugged the sheet around her body and sat on the edge of the bed.

He filled in some of the blanks. "You run a very large, very successful investment firm. A very important lady, since your father died."

"My father's dead?" Lise shut her eyes. "I have no memory of that. I suppose I take care of my mother now. She's such a wuss. I always wanted her to be stronger to him for me. What about my brother? Where is he?"

"You'll have to fill in that part yourself." He stood up and stretched. "Money went missing. Somebody died, you said so yourself."

"How does that all fit together?"

"A cool $885,000. You were the account manager. Do you remember?"

"What!" She stood up. "I don't know if I know. That's a fair amount of money." Lise turned on the shower and stepped inside the tub. He followed her into the bathroom.

"Can I help?" He slipped inside the curtains and reached for the soap. "Maybe I can massage it out of you."

"Funny man, I'm serious." She turned to face him. "*Ahem*, close quarters in here."

"The better to soap you with, my dear."

"Your hands feel good." She closed your eyes and leaned her head back under the water.

"*Uh-oh*, the soldier is back," he grinned.

"Is that why they have that picture on the box? The Trojan?"

"It's a male thing." His hands began to knead her shoulders and then move lower. His lips found hers as the water poured over their bodies. "Ah, look what I found." His hand turned like a magician's. "See, nothing up my sleeve. Oh, sorry, no sleeves." Instead of a coin, he rolled a packaged condom across the back of his knuckles.

***

"Do you have any newspapers about the story?" They were in the kitchen, eating again. "Maybe if I could read about it, I'd remember."

"Am I boring you with my food, ocean scenery or is it the sex? Why do you want to ruin the moment?"

"I have to know. Don't you understand?"

"Nope. Your Type-A personality is kicking in again. You know that, don't you? The papers are biased. I want you to remember everything yourself. No help." He wore the Greek captain's cap again.

"You are not my Robinson Crusoe and I am not your girl Friday. I have a job and a home and a mother who is probably worried silly. I don't know why Teddy's not in the picture."

"You want cheese on your potato?" He fetched the salsa and salad.

She pinched her baked potato. "Mine's done. Are you listening to me?"

He added mango sorbet to the tea glasses. “Yeah. You will love this combination. Hot and cold, spicy and mild, sort of like us. Don’t get your panties in a snit. Oh, no panties today, eh? Anyway, you’ll figure this all out. You’ve made good progress.” He kissed her cheek. “Yummy, but we won’t go there, not until later tonight.” He looked very smug. “I must paint the rest of the day.”

“When will Ella come again?”

“She won’t be here for a couple of days. She made a couple of special trips after you came here.”

“I’d like some newspapers and a few other things. Are the police looking for me?”

“Yes. They think you took the money and ran. I’m sure the bank and the police will want to talk to you. But if you don’t remember anything, how can you make them believe?”

“I feel like I need to do something. All I’ve done so far is walk and eat and - well…” She met his gaze.

“But you do them very nicely if I’m any judge. I think the more you relax, your memory will come back and this case will be solved, mademoiselle.”

“So I’m not married?”

“I wouldn’t have made love to you if you belonged to someone else. I do have standards.”

“You won’t tell me my name?”

“Nope.”

“Where I live?”

“Sorry.”

"Was there anything about a death mentioned in the robbery?"

"They haven't called it a robbery, only missing money and no death, but the television newscasters are giving you a lot of coverage and a lot of suspicions."

"I feel like I'm on that television show, "Jeopardy." I have some answers but not all the questions to piece it together. There's nothing else you will share."

"You seem to be coming along fine without my intrusions." He took a bite of his salad and chewed thoughtfully. He wondered when she would remember the part about her brother's death. After lunch, Grayson returned to his easel and paints. Lise washed the dishes. She called the dog and selected a hat from the rack. "I'm going out. I'll be back before dark.

"Why don't you stay around here?"

"Because I don't want to bother you and there's nothing to do here while you paint."

"Try painting. I'll put up an easel for you."

"Don't be difficult. I'll be out of your hair, oops. Sorry."

He laughed. "It's growing back. You said so yourself. They say it grows back thicker and curlier." He pretended to curl a moustache.

"We're out of here. Come, Casey."

She looked back and waved when she saw him watching from the window. Her legs burned from the fast walk to the end of his island. Because the tide was running especially low, Lise waded across the inlet wanting to return to the house in the woods. She circled the gardens and entered the clearing from the front. The doors were bolted shut, but she tried them anyway. She looked carefully into every window. The window screens prevented her from testing the locks. She was about to leave when she heard a boat's engine. She grabbed the dog's collar, pulled him towards the garage and crouched down, peering towards the driveway.

No one came. She slid to the ground beside a tree and drew the dog close. She was afraid to move and afraid not to. It seemed like a long time before she unfolded and stepped out into the yard.

A man with long curly dark hair, dressed in a uniform white shirt and trousers came around the house. "No! Go 'way. No, no, no. You're not s'posed to be here." He screamed at her. Dark hair fell across his face and a scowl screwed his mouth. His communication skills, though primitive, sent the message loud and clear. She didn't wait for an introduction. Lise grabbed the dog's collar and pulled him back between the shrubberies.

"You're trespassing. If you come back, I'll find you. You'll be sorry!" He hurled a rock in her direction and continued to shout as she ran deeper into the woods.

Her nightmare revived except this time, she was awake and running. Pulling the dog, she forced herself into the undergrowth to hide, stumbling on roots in the scrub. Branches scratched her arms and legs. Casey strained against her. From deep inside, a yell surfaced. “I don’t want to go back. I’ve had enough. Leave me alone!”

She had no idea why those precise words came out. Her hands shook and she could hear her heart beating in her ears. Her stomach clutched into a tight fist as she hid in the undergrowth. He hadn’t followed her. After listening to the woods for a few minutes, she crept out.

Threading her belt through the dog’s collar, she pulled him along on her makeshift leash. Her side ached from the exertion. When Lise reached the narrow channel between the islands, she plunged into the water. The incoming tide pushed the water up to her chest. Her shoulder screamed in pain when the tide wretched the swimming dog from her grasp.

Lise lost her footing and let the water carry her. She swam on her side, riding the surge along the shore until her feet found bottom again. Casey followed her up to the top of a sand hill. She slid into a sandy dip, leaning against the warm sand. Did she hear something? Her ragged breathing made her mouth dry. She tasted the salt on her lips. Sand stuck on her wet skin; her ears hummed. The warm sand seduced her into folding her arms around her legs and she slept.

THIRTEEN

Grayson found her nestled in the sand, sleeping like a bird, her arms curled around her body. Fearing the worst, he said. "Lise, wake up. Are you hurt? Talk to me."

She opened her eyes and stared.

"Lise, can you hear me? Casey came to the house with your belt buckled through his collar. I was afraid you left me."

She squinted into the late afternoon sun, "Grayson, Minnow."

He held her head. "Yes, it's me! Do you remember me? Us?"

She nodded; a pleasing smile broke across her face.

"Thank God, you didn't forget that, us." His lips brushed the sand from her cheek as he kissed her. "What happened?"

"I went back to that house and the tide came in." Lise clutched his shirt. "There was a man there. He was horrid, screaming and throwing rocks. Is Casey alright?"

"Yes, Casey's fine. What about you? Can you stand?"

Grayson pulled her to her feet. "Why can't you stay on this side of the inlet? Why do you have to wander off island?" He rubbed her hands to increase circulation and catch her attention. "Lise, promise me you won't go back unless I'm with you." Grayson searched her face. "It's dangerous."

"Yes, I can see that now. I'm sorry," she said. "Why do I keep fazing out? The dizziness and drowsiness has to mean something." She reached for his hand. "Do you know if I have some horrible sickness? Am I going to die?"

"No, I think it's the stress from family and work catching up with you. Fresh salt air also has a power that allows you to heal. I've experienced that myself." He turned her toward his body. "Promise me you won't go back there. I'll take you there, myself. We'll go together."

"Ok, I won't go back without you." She looked back across the inlet. "When will you take me back? I feel like I've been there a long time ago."

"I have to paint!" He watched her frown as she looked across the inlet. "We'll go back tomorrow afternoon if you let me paint in the morning. Is that soon enough for you?" Grayson's mind whirled. *She saw Pauli. He must have been as frightened as she was.*

***

The next morning, after breakfast, Lise stood at the door. "Would you mind if I join you on your walk?"

Torn between wanting solace and wanting her close, he said, "You may come." His arm reached around her as he kissed her forehead. "We both have to get used to this togetherness." He reached for a hat and gave her one, too. "How's the memory? Anything new to report?"

"My father was a strict disciplinarian. My mother rarely interfered. In fact, she was pretty useless, one of those mindless blondes that attract so many of you men." She reached over and punched him gently in the ribs. "I remember that much. I remember my grandmother's house and my brother Teddy was a jolly fellow, always laughing and kidding us both. I remember him laughing and pointing. He must have been awful to pal around with."

"We fished and swam together. I knew the best fishing holes and could fix his motor when he needed it fixed." Grayson tried to keep up a good face although talking about Ted annoyed him.

"I used to follow you and watch you when you both went out in the boat. I also remembered being pushed on the dock at that house. I know I've been there." She leaned her head against his arm as they walked. "Can you tell me more?"

"*Hmm*?" Grayson remembered that Ted took every opportunity to embarrass Pauli. When Pauli, Grayson's brother, was a boy, he understood he was slower than other children were, but he accepted his handicap. Grayson marveled in remembering that Pauli had called Teddy's meanness and poor manners another kind of handicap. He was miles and years away as she talked. When she stopped walking and looked at him, he drew his mind back to her.

"Oh no, I think it's better if you remember it all for yourself, but that sounds about right. You were right about your parents and that Ted was a character." He didn't want to break her bubble of admiration for Ted, yet.

"This is what I know. I remember being out on a boat fishing, swimming, sunburn, the smell of Noxzema, old dried shrimp we used as bait, sailor hats and being happy." She stooped to pick up a shell and turned it over in her hand. "We had a little catboat. I could sail it myself."

"You did." He watched her fingers scrape along the ridges of the cockle shell. As she brushed sand from the shell, he plotted a new picture in his mind. He'd paint it after the one he started that morning. It would be of a girl on the sand with a shell. "You're an inspiration. You know that?"

"Why do you say that?" She grabbed his hand and began to walk again.

"I look at you and I see another painting build."

"Is that how you do it? You visualize something and have it all drawn out before you start or do you get an idea and then it grows on the canvas?"

"Both." He kissed her hand and felt the sand grit between her fingers. "Come on now, you're slowing my progress."

"You can't tell me about the money thing?" She tossed the shell back into the water. "Was it cash or wire transfer, company check, embezzled over a period of time or all of a sudden?"

"It was a one time thing, lots of money. Ring any bells?"

"No." She shook her head. "I can't imagine...wait." Her top lip disappeared as her bottom teeth raked it. "There was one large check. Was that the one?"

"I wouldn't know, but I'd like to be sure before I let you resurface and they grab you up. Do you think that's who's chasing you, in your dreams, the bank people?"

"No. It's something bigger, like -- oh, I don't know." She pressed both hands into her stomach. "I can feel the turmoil here, when I think about going back."

They walked further along the beach returning to his home within the hour. She sat on the porch when he went inside. A few minutes later, he came to the door.

"Come in." He chugged the last bit of water from his glass and crunched his ice from his glass. "I've got something for you."

"Oh, goody, I love surprises." She took a long swallow from her own glass and followed. "Well, this is interesting." Her hand reached out as she felt the gessoed mason board on a new easel. "It's grainy. Does that hold the paint better?" She stood beside her easel, watching as Grayson picked up his brush and dipped it into the brush cleaner. He worked the bristles back and forth softening them. "It gives a nice texture to the painting. Try it. You may find you're good at it." He didn't turn to watch her. "Sometimes I use just a piece of gessoed board to catch my ideas. It's cheaper than stretched canvas and easier to paint on."

Lise selected three different shades of blue and squished out a glob of each. Her uneasiness about painting disappeared as she played with the colors and brushes. She chose a wide, stiff-bristled brush and made strokes across her panel. "I suppose I did this, too, and you aren't going to tell me."

"Hush. Don't talk. Let the brush do your storytelling." His own painting was forming already, a woman in the sand holding a shell. Grayson outlined ocean and dunes in pale strokes. Soft illusions arose on the canvas as clouds drifted over dunes on a peaceful day.

"Very nice." She peeked over his shoulder, admiring his skill. "Oops, sorry. I'm not looking. I'm not looking. You won't hear any further peeps." She painted a crude picture, a boat on the water and clouds in the sky. Her mind drifted as she applied layers of paint, changing the smooth water into a rough sea by adding whitecaps and depth to the waves, a few seagulls whirled overhead. As she darkened the sky, she remembered taking off her watch and rings and putting them in a canister by the kitchen sink. *Where was I?*

She saw herself pull back her hair into a pony tail. Her mind kept rewinding and playing the scene repeatedly while her hand continued to paint. The sun was shining, but there was a storm. She posed a lightening strike on the horizon. "I remember the waves flattened by the force of the storm. I lost my rudder and the wind grabbed the sheets out of my hand. The boom swung and I went overboard. I fell overboard after hitting my head. The boom swayed as I got up…" She looked at her empty hands to see if the sheets had burned stripes on her palms as they whipped from her grasp. She remembered the sting of the rope burns.

She didn't know he was standing behind her when he reached over and took her brush. "Well, that solves one of your mysteries."

"It was like dreaming while I was standing on my feet." She looked at her painting. "Is this what happened? I got caught up in the storm and thrown overboard."

"It wouldn't be the first time someone tangled with a storm off our coast."

When she looked at him, his eyebrows rose with that little furrow on his forehead. She grabbed up a putty knife and angrily smeared a swath of yellow across her picture. "I'm a better sailor than that! If the rudder hadn't come off, it wouldn't have happened." She looked at him. "The rudder sheared. I couldn't steer. Nimbus clouds, it was frightening. No, they were mammus clouds! I've never seen them before except in pictures. The wind was screaming."

"There was a bad storm. The sky turned black but I kept painting that evening."

"Did you find my boat?"

"No, it must have drifted further along the coast or sunk. In that storm and with the Gulf Stream, it could be to Hatteras by now. If someone finds it, they'll know who owned it by looking at the numbers on the bow."

"It's so frustrating. I lost my Uncle Eddie's boat. Ohmygosh. It's my boat. It was in my name."

"I can tell you that someone noticed your boat was missing last week. The caretaker thought the boat was towed away by the storm. In your home town there's a rumor you faked your disappearance."

"See, that's what gets me mad. You know things, but you don't share them. Until something like this happens." She went over to the couch and dropped down. "It really pisses me off when you do this."

"Settle down. You let me paint uninterrupted for two hours. Thank-you-very-much. You inspired it and I have a ways to go, but it's coming along. No?"

Her breathing returned to normal as she gazed at his latest work. A line of morning glories draped along sand fencing. A woman with bare feet and painted toenails sat in the sandy foreground. "That's not me! My nails are paler." She held out her toes to prove her point. "Does your painting tell more about me than mine?"

"I really don't know." He walked out the front door this time and performed a series of stretches and twists, relaxing his shoulders.

She made them each a glass of tea and brought one back for him, when he returned to his painting. "Shall we paint over it?" She nodded at her work. "Or am I to do a series of bad paintings to illustrate my plight here on your island?"

"I taught an art therapy class once, filling in for a friend. I still teach occasionally. I'm surprised this all came out. Now that you are conscious of what you did, it may not work as well, but," he took her painting down and replaced it with another empty board, "let's see if you come up with anything else."

"I'd rather give it a break. I think I'll clean house. Would you paint me doing that?" She tiptoed over and kissed him on the lips. When his arms went around enclosing her in his grip, she said. "Nope, none of that, mister. We both know there is work to be done." She flipped her body around, still in his arms. "Now say goodbye to the nice lady who is going to wash your countertops and clean out your refrigerator." She felt his lips on her neck and purred before tearing herself away.

"Before you came, I didn't change or clean things much."

"Well I'm glad you changed your habits. Now back to the canvas, sir."

She counted off four-five days being on his island. She remembered her family home, a strict father and her playful older brother. She remembered forms and stacks of paper, her secretary named Millie, but nothing about the missing money.

She filled the sink with soapy water and started to wash down the cabinets. She hung the cleaning rags on the line to dry then busied herself inside the house straightening things and sweeping out the sand. Upstairs she swept off the deck and pulled back the curtains. She returned to the kitchen and piled sandwich fillings on hoagie rolls for lunch. “You like lettuce and tomato on your sandwich?”

“Yes, I do.”

“See, now other couples have to go through all those dating games. We seem to be getting all the rudiments of likes and dislikes without too many trials and errors.”

He didn’t respond.

“Are you learning everything you need to know about me?” She rambled on, “I guess we are finding out about me together. It’s an interesting exercise. It’s like one of those business rah-rah meetings they have for corporate managers, where they go off and find out things about themselves.”

“Did you go to one of them?”

“I guess so if I know about them so well. Team stuff, macho man and all for one, that kind of stuff you hear about. I think I even had to jump off a tower somewhere. A lot of good it does me here.”

She sliced a ripe tomato on their sandwiches and used pickles and chips to garnish their plates. “Come and get it.” While they sat on the back porch, the cleaning cloths fluttered in the breeze.

“So what do you think?”

“About what?”

“I was saying that we took a shortcut to getting acquainted. We didn’t have to meet at work or go on a blind date to test the waters. I think it’s the ideal way for a couple to get to know one another, live together in close quarters and find out if they are compatible. Cut out all that other stuff.

Force us to live together. It's like a test and saves a lot of time, if you ask me."

He continued chewing his sandwich and didn't add one comment to her monologue on their meeting and mating. She shrugged, used to his non-answers. It was late afternoon when she heard a boat horn coming from the sound side of the island.

"Ella's here. Since you've met her, want to come?" He handed her a straw hat and pulled on his own wide-brimmed one.

"Yeah, she may have brought me some more goodies, right?" She hoped the pregnancy test would be among them.

"Maybe she'll have news about you." He marched over the dune with both dog and Lise following.

Two people were in the boat. Grayson slowed for a moment and then reached for her hand. "Come on I want you to meet someone. I had no idea she would bring him but now is as good a time as any."

Lise recognized the other character immediately. The man staring at her from the boat was the same one who screamed and threw rocks at the island house. Her feet dragged in the sand.

"Hello, hello," the stranger called out to Grayson. "Who's the lady?" His sing-song voice continued his greeting.

"Pauli, this is Lise. Lise, this is Ella's son, Pauli." Grayson stood back to watch her.

Pauli's tone and repetition reminded Lise of Downs Syndrome children she had known, but the older man's face looked like anyone's. He was a good looking man, older than Grayson. Pauli stood still and didn't move as she watched him.

"No, not nice to stare. Mama, she's staring." His high strained voice and moving hands displayed his anxiety. "I know you. I saw you. You aren't supposed to be there. No one goes there but Pauli and Ella."

"Pauli," Lise reached out to him, but he jerked away. "I'm glad to meet you. You gave me a scare yesterday." Her voice continued to soothe the frightened man. "Can we be friends? I'd like to be friends. Please, be my friend, won't you?" She continued to hold her hand as if she were bribing a wayward puppy.

He looked closer at her face and pointed again. "Mama, it's An--! Oh right, mum's the word." Pauli stopped his hand jerking and stood still. He looked at her hand and reached out to her.

"I wanted you to meet my son." Ella put her hand on Pauli's shoulder.

"So you're Ella's son. I'm very pleased to make your acquaintance." This time when she held out her hand, he shook the tips of her fingers, then grasped her hand in his wide grip.

"Well, I was coming anyway to bring you a few things, like you asked me." She winked at Lise under the brim of her hat. "You said you wanted some under-things. I thought you might want a swimsuit, too, since you're here. Mr. Armstrong, here's your supplies and I threw in a couple of newspapers. We're taking a boat ride around the islands. Lise, want to come? Mr. Armstrong can carry this stuff back up to the house. No sense unpacking her things, son, it's all girly stuff, if you get my drift."

Grayson gave her a queer nod and took the bags. "No problem, I have a painting to work on." He grabbed another small canvas bag of supplies and mail, lifting them from the boat.

Ella pulled on Lise's arm as she stepped into the boat. "I was hoping to get you and Pauli together." A coughing spell overwhelmed Ella. It stopped only after she bent over and slowed her breathing. "There, that's better. I need something to take my mind off smoking. Boats and fishing is all I know, so we decided to close the store and take off this afternoon." She pointed for Lise to take her seat forward in the boat beside her son. The handsome man with the childlike expression helped her to her seat.

FOURTEEN

"Pauli, tell Miss Lise what you do on that island. I'll sit back here and steer while you two get acquainted." The woman sat on her shelf and flipped her hand at her son. "Go on, she won't bite. Talk to her." The boat turned away from shore as Ella settled her back against the transom. An old boat cushion softened her seat.

Lise waved goodbye at Grayson and watched him disappear over the dunes. "I'm sorry. I didn't mean to upset you yesterday." Lise's voice barely carried over the sound of the engine.

The long-haired man said, "It's alright. You just scared me. No one ever goes there but troublemakers. I thought you were a troublemaker. I cut the grass and weed for the owners. Sometimes I replace a window glass when they get broke. Troublemakers aren't supposed to be there. They spray paint, too, or try to break inside. My job is to watch out for them and clean up their messes. That's what I do."

"You have a lot of responsibilities."

“I got my own business. I fix things.” He seemed to relax as he talked, his fingers fidgeted with each other, but his voice was clear.

“You take a boat and come over often, by yourself?”

“Yeah, I drive this boat and I fish. I know my way around these waters. Daddy taught me all about fishing. I help Mama with her store. I’m not a dummy. I can drive.” He smiled, pleased with himself. “I have a van so I haul my tools and stuff. I have a white van. I bought it with my own money.” He settled more into the bench seat beside her and braced his arm reaching across Lise’s back to the side of the boat.

“A business man, with a good head on his shoulders, too.” Lise looked back at Ella.

The older woman nodded and pushed out her bottom lip. “He also helps at the gallery, don’t you Pauli?” Her fingers went up and hunting for the missing pack of cigarettes that usually bulged out her top pocket.

“Yes. I clean up for Miss Josie and help her hang pictures. She has lots of pictures. A lot are -- Mr. Armstrong’s. I like his the best. Her store is downtown. Have you ever been there?”

“No. I don’t remember being there. I’d remember you, Pauli, if I saw you before, wouldn’t I?”

“Mama said I couldn’t tell you anything about you. It’s hard, but I’m not going to mess up.” His face formed a smirk as he glanced back at his mother.

"You're doing right, Pauli. Missy, we've been instructed not to give you any help. You need to find your own story. Sorry, but we're under strict orders." She started coughing again.

Pauli spoke softly so only Lise could hear. "Mama says she's going to be with Daddy. I'll miss her."

"What?" Lise leaned close to the man. "What did you say?"

He nodded. "Soon, she said soon." He wiped his face with the back of his shirt sleeve and nodded his head.

Lise closed her mouth when she realized it was open. She had noticed Ella's wheezing. "I had no idea it was this bad." She placed her hand on his shoulder. "I'm sorry, Pauli." She sat back on her seat and wondered what else they knew that they hadn't told her.

"Hold on, we're coming to the inlet." Pauli grabbed Lise's arm that was closer and held her tight. Lise jostled against him but Pauli didn't flinch when she bumped him repeatedly as the boat entered the inlet. His mother maneuvered the boat through the trough and around to the ocean side of the island. The sea was choppy and the bounce of the waves had Pauli nudging her occasionally as his body moved next to hers. His strong arm behind her made her feel safer in the rough waters. Her eyes scanned for the life jackets. She didn't want to repeat her last boat ride in the ocean.

"Sometimes we come out and fish together, Mama and me. We're both good fishermen. Have you been fishing lately?"

It was hard to hang onto the boat and conversation, but Lise grabbed at Pauli's words as the boat plowed through the ocean.

"I like to fish. I haven't been lately."

Pauli leaned over to spoke above the motor, but Ella couldn't hear. "I remember you from when you were a little girl. You were nice to me. I liked you. We fished sometimes. Your brother was mean. He teased me. Mama told me not to let your brother bother me. Your brother's handicap," he made sure he said the word carefully, "I think his handicap was he was mean. But you know that, don't you?" His eyebrows went up into his bangs and he grinned. "You were a nice little girl."

Lise looked back to see if Ella heard Pauli. Her hand was on the wheel but her eyelids fluttered in a quiet sleep. The boat seemed to steer itself. "Yes, Pauli, Teddy could be a bother. It's ok. I remembered that."

She half-lied to him as she held his hand. She heard Ella rouse herself a short while later. As the boat turned towards the shallow side of the island, Lise searched her mind to remember Teddy's meanness. Vague memories began to surface. When they reached the shallows near Grayson's dock, Lise turned to see Ella's gaze resting on her older son.

"I'll be bringing out Mr. Armstrong's stuff if anything happens to Mama." Pauli nudged Lise's arm. "I plan on taking over the store when Mama gets so she can't do it any longer."

"He's gonna take over the store. Did he tell you? I'm getting tired of all this running around. You need anything, you can trust him."

"I'm sure you'll do a good job, Pauli." Lise was startled with the frankness of the pair.

Ella pointed to the dock. "Can you make it from here or you want me to blow the horn and get Mr. Armstrong back?"

"I'll be ok." Lise hopped up on the dock. "I enjoyed meeting you, Pauli. Ella, you take care of yourself. Are you seeing a doctor? Are you doing what he says?"

"Honey, a doctor can't do much for me now. I'm just enjoying what I can while I can do it. Don't worry about me. You'll get back your memory. I can see it all coming back." She fiddled with the steering wheel a moment. "Say, do you still like to fish? Maybe we can go fishing sometime."

"Yes. I'd like that. Grayson is too busy to take me fishing. I hope to see you next time you come this way. Thank you – for everything."

Lise watched as Pauli shifted back to take the wheel from his mother. Ella steadied the boat as it gently bumped against the dock. "Earlier, he was mighty upset. Glad we settled that." She nodded at her son. "I'm glad you got a chance to be acquainted. There's no call to frighten each other again."

"Water the plants and come right back. I go there to water the plants and come right back." Pauli repeated.

"Sorry, Missy, if he upset you."

Lise regretted going to the island house and frightening Pauli. After climbing over the sand dunes, she found Grayson painting in his usual stance. “He seems better. I’m sorry. I didn’t know.” Lise tugged her bag of clothes off the table in the kitchen hanging them over her shoulder.

“If you had stayed on *this* island it wouldn’t have happened.”

She heard anger in his tone. “Does that mean we can’t go over there this evening?”

He hesitated a moment. “No, I said we’d go and we will.”

Lise took her things upstairs. She tucked the pregnancy test between the mattress and bedspring. She tore open the sack of underwear to discover her new granny drawers. Lise trashed the plastic wrapping as Grayson came up the steps. She held a pair of her new white panties up to her front. “You like?” She batted her eye lashes and swayed her hips.

“Very - serviceable, I guess is the word.” He shut the bathroom door behind him.

“I guess we could always use them for brush wipes when I wear them out!” She went over and banged on the door jokingly. “Are you going to keep me prisoner until I wear them out?”

“You aren’t my prisoner.” Her fist landed on his chest when he opened the bathroom door. “I thought we got over that detail.” He stepped aside. “Better go now or you’ll be looking for a bush before we get back." His grim expression told Lise he was in no joking mood.

"Seems all I do today is say I'm sorry and try to keep out of trouble."

As Grayson rowed, Lise scooped out the water that seeped into the craft. The dog sat in the bow. "I'm interrupting your day again. It's just that the house has a drawing power."

Grayson took several pulls on the oars before responding. "I understand that the house is important to you. That's why I'm taking you there." He rowed them across the inlet and around to the sound side of the other island so that they came to the dock at the foot of the driveway. "Give me that line and I'll tie it." Grayson stood and helped her climb up on the dock. The dog jumped out of the boat, swam ashore and met them on the gravel path. They stopped to put on their shoes.

"It's a good-looking home. Do you remember anything else about it?"

"Do you have a key?"

He raised his faint eyebrows. "Yes." She could see eyebrows now for sure. He reached into his pocket, pulled out a key and tossed it to her. She caught it and trotted to the front door.

"Thank you." Lise pushed the door inwards. "I know I've been here before." She smelled hickory smoke from the fireplace. She felt like she was walking into an old familiar dream. The coolness of the home enveloped her as she walked across the wooden floors."

"I heard they used the wood from old tobacco barns to build this." Grayson toed the floor with his boat shoes. Dark paneling covered the walls flanking the fireplace.

Pots and pans hung from a kitchen rack, but no food was in the pantry or refrigerator. Stainless steel commercial appliances lined one wall. Apprehensive, she waited for a memory to return. Her fingers felt the cool surfaces of the dark stone-topped counters. "It's almost dreary, not enough light here. It needs a couple of sky lights, don't you think?"

Lise peeked under the sheets that draped across the plaid couches and wing-backed chairs. "It's a man's home," she surmised. "See the bold colors, lack of knick-knacks on the shelves and heaviness of the furniture. Am I right?" She walked back into the kitchen area and stared out the wide row of windows. "The kitchen is the only thing I remember. It's not my house. Who owns it?"

He shook his head.

Grayson leaned his back against the front door as he watched her enter the master bedroom and guestrooms. "You have to answer that one. Sorry."

"I'm drawing a blank here. Nothing comes to mind." She hugged her arms to her body and walked through once more, touching the cool counter tops and stainless steel appliances. She tested the spigots by turning them on and off. "The water is turned on. Oh, Pauli waters the plants." Lise sat at the barstool and put her face down on the counter top. "*Hmm*, I feel like I'm in a dream that isn't ending well." She stroked the mantel and pulled the sheet back over the couch.

She bent to pick up a long red hair. “Look what I found. There must be a woman around.” She held up the strand like a trophy. “Our man had company for a while or the red-headed ghost is shedding her locks.”

Grayson hid his mixed emotions. He thought it was probably her hair, shed years before. He felt like a trapeze artist holding her ankles so she could glimpse her former life.

“It’s a comfortable house, but needs a woman’s touch. I’d have cut flowers all around and use accent colors on a wall or two. I love the gardens. I bet when they were put in, it was grand.” She walked out. He followed, pulling the door shut. “I’m done here. Mind if I walk around a bit more?”

“This is your visit. Get it all out of your system.” He gestured towards the grounds but sat on the swing while she poked about the out buildings. She returned with a question on her face.

“Do you have keys for the padlocks on the other buildings?”

“We’ve intruded enough, don’t you think?”

She shrugged and followed him back towards the dock. Their feet made crunches on the gravel as they walked.

“My brother owns this, doesn’t he?” The idea shot into her mind as if the missing sibling suddenly appeared at her side. “Why isn’t he taking better care of this?’

“Yes, but he --”

She interrupted, "I knew it. It felt right. He won't care that I'm here. Let's borrow a jet ski and then you won't have to row us back. Let's do it." She pleaded with him.

"No, we need to return to my island before it gets dark. Perhaps we'll come back another time. I promise -- when you remember more." He hopped down into the dinghy and held up his hand. She removed her sandals and followed.

"Is Teddy a bully?" She dumped a scoop of water over the side of the boat as he rowed. "Is he mean to you or Pauli?" She shuddered. "I feel like he's watching from behind a tree or something."

Grayson continued to row. "Not any more. He doesn't do it anymore."

"Good. I guess all little boys have a mean streak in them sometimes. Didn't you?"

"No. I never did."

She hesitated, not speaking again until they reached shore. The first star came out before they could drag the dinghy into the shed and stow the gear. She put her arm around him and snuggled up close.

"Maybe I'll bring out the big boat later this week." Grayson's mind seemed to be elsewhere. "With the weather getting warmer we need to have it out at the dock."

***

She rolled over and her hand brushed his shoulder as they lay in bed. "Are you thinking about your show? Is it a big one?"

She felt his hand smooth her hair. “It’s a big one, but they are all big these days. I have some people coming from a New York gallery.” He ran a finger down her spine. ”They come from a lot of places.”

She turned and spoke over her shoulder. “Are you famous? I mean, well do your paintings get you enough to live on?”

He chuckled and pulled her close.

“I choose to live the way I do. I hope you choose to live this way, too.”

“But I have to go home. I mean, I have a business and a mother and God only knows whatever else as responsibilities. Grayson, I have to leave.”

“I knew one day you’d say that.” His lips stilled on her shoulder.

“Let’s get back to my original question. Are you a famous artist?”

“You said you didn’t know any live ones, remember?” He nuzzled her neck, "You wouldn't know me." He pulled her into his arms spooning her body into his. "I have to go away next month."

She turned her head kissing him on his arm. "I'll be gone by then. It doesn't matter." She felt his grip tighten. "Tell me about where and when you’ll be gone?"

"I teach workshops for special needs children and adults."

"Really? How did you get involved in that?"

"It started one spring in Nantucket. Someone found out I had an interest and they invited me up to put on a program."

"You do, because of Pauli?"

"Yes." His hand began to move upward. "I enjoy it and it helps me to gain a better perspective on my art."

"How long will you be gone?"

"Six weeks all together. I have to fly to Europe also."

"What?" She grabbed his hand to keep it still. His lips froze on her neck.

"Some art collecting baroness from Spain visited my workshop for children one year. Evidently, she has a Down's syndrome child and he was in the class. She's put together an entire month of classes for the handicapped in various cities in Europe -- London, Paris, Zurich and Barcelona. There'll be several of us going."

"Grayson, you *are* famous! You've been leading me on. I thought you were a poor wretch, meagerly working out of your grandparent's abandoned home to survive on a few sales."

"My paintings sell very well. You, my dear woman, are sleeping with a wealthy, new-money kind of man, bald, but very wealthy."

"Are you telling me you live on an island without a lot of stuff because you choose not to flaunt it?"

His lips nibbled her shoulder. "I survive very nicely." He kissed her shoulder and one hand caressed her. "In fact, one sold painting is all I need for my living expenses for six months or a whole year."

She threw his hands away. "You lied to me!" She rolled away and turned to face him. "How could you make me think you were some poor fool painting away on a deserted island because he can't afford to live on the mainland?"

"I didn't lie to you. I left a few things out." He rolled over and reached for his shorts on the floor. "I also have a home on the mainland, new information for you to turn over in your angry jumbled mind."

"This is what I hate. I ask you questions that you refuse to answer. Then, I'm upset with you when I find out the answers."

He pulled on his shorts and zipped the fly. "I'm not arguing with you, Lise. It's not worth it. I'm going downstairs to paint."

“But don’t you understand. There’s this mess of missing money and that’s got to be about the chasing that I dream about.”

He said nothing more.

***

Sometime after midnight, when he finally came to bed, she was sleeping soundly. He rolled towards her and pulled her into his arms. She nuzzled his arm and continued to sleep despite his trail of kisses along her neck.

FIFTEEN

They breakfasted on the porch on sweet rolls, hot tea and coffee and then walked. He quietly painted as she sat on the couch. "Are you angry with me?" Lise asked.

"No, I'm not angry with you. Whatever mood I'm in it's not helping me paint."

"You seem angry. Is there someone else who is making you angry?"

"Can we move this conversation somewhere else?" He put his brush down and stared at her. "Josie will be coming over in her own fashion sometime this week. I need to have as many completed paintings as I can before she shows up. She's my agent and she owns a gallery in town. I'm lucky to have her but she can be, well, you'll see." He wiped his head with a hand. "You won't like her. I'm not sure I do but she knows how to sell."

"A she?"

"*Uh-huh.*"

"Is she pretty?"

"What difference does that make?"

"I'm trying to picture you with another woman." She blushed, "I mean anyone else for that matter." She walked to her easel, borrowed one of his brushes and added a line of color to a bucket of flowers she'd painted earlier. "Is there someone else, like before I was here?"

"That's a stupid question. The way I am, I didn't think another woman would ever look at me. It's one of the reasons I liked my solitude." He picked up his brush and dabbed at the canvas. "There's no one else."

"Good."

Pushing aside the brim of his cap, he readjusted it so the bill shadowed the back of his neck.

"I don't see how you do this. How do you get the leaves to look right?"

"It's an acquired talent."

She turned to look at his picture, pushed her bottom lip out and held her head at an angle studying the painting.

"What's wrong?"

"I think you're painting my grandmother's house. Are you?"

"No."

"You're a friend of my brother's? He was fifteen years older than I am." She stood with her hands on her hips. "How old are you Grayson?"

"You're going there again, Lise. I wouldn't say your brother and I were friends. I don't want to talk about it."

"Fine." She dropped her brush into his jar of brush cleaner. "You have secrets, my good man. I wish you'd share them so I wouldn't feel so left out."

"Not now, later. I have it from a good authority the sooner you remember all this, the better you will accept your life."

Lise walked out the door mumbling. "Maybe I don't want to remember my old life. Maybe I'm trying to forget it." She stomped her feet and slid them into her sandals. "Come here, dog."

Casey pulled himself out from under the porch where he slept in the cool sand. He shook himself and lifted a back leg to scratch.

"Want to go for another never-ending walk?" She headed down to the sound with the dog close behind. During the past week, she had circumnavigated the entire island. She knew its birds, ponies, and quirks of the tide. The bits and pieces of her prior life that she remembered weren't that happy, but maybe she could change that. Once she got her memory back, she knew she had to leave the island. He hadn't asked her to stay.

Her mind raced over the conversations of the past week, comparing him to her storybook characters. Now she compared him to Peter Pan. She wanted him to grow up, take responsibility for his emotions and claim his affection. *He has to like me, but does he love me? Why doesn't he flat out ask me to stay on his island? He hasn't even said anything about me coming back here later when I get this money mess straightened out. I want marriage and children. Didn't he say he wanted children? He hasn't mentioned wanting to be married again.*

She picked up a stick and threw it in frustration. The dog galloped off and promptly brought it back and dropped it at her foot, her sandaled foot. *He shod me. He painted my toes. Why can't a man say what he's feeling? Do I love him? I don't know who I am. How can I know I love him?*

Her new sandals were squishing in the wet sand, sinking deeper with each step. A crying sound broke into her thoughts. At first, she thought it was a bird crying, but as she listened, the cry became more frantic. Lise and the dog jogged toward the noise. A herd of horses was grazing near the shore. Her gaze shifted. Near the reed-choked shoreline, the painted colt struggled in the mud. His hind quarters sank deeper every time he jerked. His tiny mud covered hooves and forelegs couldn't find a surface to bear his weight.

Lise knew she couldn't help the colt alone, but Grayson could come. But would he return in time? Lise raced back to the house. Soaked with sweat by the time she arrived, she called for him then sank into the rocker.

He came to the door, paintbrush in hand.

"Colt! Stuck in the mud, can't get out," she gasped.

Grayson returned with something for her to drink and a damp towel. He pushed her hair back and wiped her face and neck.

"Not me, I'll be fine. We have to help that colt, please." Distraught, she remembered another child, "Oh my God, Grayson. I lost a child, didn't I? I lost a child!"

"Stop! What are you saying?"

"You don't have time to humor me. Go!"

"Catch your breath. Tell me where the colt is." She explained about the time and place they first saw the painted colt on their first dinghy ride. It seemed like months, but it was just over a week.

"Stay here. I've done this before."

She had never ventured inside his various outbuildings. On occasion, he'd bring out tools or return equipment. Her curiosity turned to surprise when he drove an all-terrain vehicle out of the larger shed. He adjusted the motor and hopped off the small four-wheeler.

"You have a little truck? What else are you hiding in there?" Grayson piled boards, rope, a blanket and an old block and tackle in the small truck bed.

With a grim face he said, "Casey, stay. You, Lise, stay and calm down."

Before Lise could answer, he spun the vehicle around. It banked onto the dunes spitting sand with its big tires. *He has a vehicle. Why didn't I know that? What else is he hiding in there?*

As her breathing returned to normal, her curiosity grew. There were three buildings on the property. The door to one stood open. Her hand felt the sun-warm combination lock as she stood outside looking in. Heat from the sun penetrated the stuffy shed and she felt like she stood at the door of an oven.

Lise walked inside to investigate. Allowing a minute for her eyes to adjust to the dark, she noted tools hung neatly along one wall, jerry jugs of different colors crowded together on a shelf and a VHF radio and battery pack at a workbench. An antenna ran up one wall. Lying beside the radio was an accordion file of papers and a cell phone with his wallet. *A cell phone, that's how he calls Ella.*

Shocked at finding out more about Grayson's secrets, Lise reached out and picked up the phone. She flipped through the bank of names and addresses. Ella and Josie were the only familiar ones she recognized. *How could he do this? He said there was no phone. Why has he lied to me*?

Her hand felt the soft leather of his wallet. A few bills, two charge cards and his driver license peeked out of one slot. She couldn't bring herself to pull the card from its slim pocket to read his name. She remembered him as Minnow and had no need to find out any more information. *Did he leave the door open for me? Is this a test?*

Test. She dropped the wallet back on his workbench and ran into the house. It was the first time she felt alone to take the pregnancy test without an interruption from Grayson. Upstairs, she pulled the smuggled box out from beneath her mattress and tore open the package. Lise sat on the bed and read the instructions. *Great, I don't know when I had my last period. How can I tell "the suggested time for testing?" Take first thing in the morning "for best results." Oh, brother. The good news is that it can tell within weeks of conception. If I was pregnant when I came to the island, this will work.*

She stuffed the papers back under the mattress and went into the bathroom. She set everything on the sink and decided the hit or miss method was probably the best. She had no watch but she carefully counted off the seconds. *Nothing. No crossed lines. Not the right color. No bells or whistles. No pregnancy.* She read the instructions again making sure she did everything right.

She put the lid down on the toilet, sat and cried. She wasn't sure if she was crying from relief or sadness. The more, she thought about it, she knew she'd done this before. This had happened before, more than once. *I wanted a child!*

A part of her life flooded into her mind, a part she wished she could forget. Her work and caring for her mother never allowed time to date seriously. Pauli said everyone was handicapped, maybe her handicap was that she couldn't attract a husband or have children. Blank spaces filled in her mind as she remembered she had foregone the regular courtship and marriage route, sought out a fertility specialist and gone to counseling to prepare for motherhood. The disappointment of being unable to conceive weighed heavily on her emotions.

That's why she was sick. When the first attempts failed, she'd taken medicine. The drugs she took to enhance her egg production had side effects that made her ill. Why was it that other women had no problem conceiving? She hid all evidence of her failure, washed her face and went downstairs. She heard the sound of his little truck coming in the distance as she wandered into the living room. She was staring at his newest painting when he tiptoed in.

The newest canvas stretched five feet across the largest easel. It was the beginning of a painting of Lise hanging sheets on the clothesline. “You took something so mundane and made it a work of art. It -- it gives me courage and peace at the same time.” The knot that had formed in her stomach released with as a warm wave of passion washed over her. He had captured her feelings of happiness and bliss, her eyes, her face in a soft wash of colors. “You never asked me if you could paint me. Well, yes, you did, but I never answered. Grayson, I think it’s your best.” She forgot her earlier sadness. “It’s absolutely wonderful, not just me. It’s the feeling I get as I look at it.”

Mud from his shorts and legs clumped on the floor. Wet sandy footprints stopped where he stood at the bottom of his stairs watching her. Did he notice a change in her stance? “You weren’t here. I started with your eyes. The rest came easily.” He liked the way her hair licked the back of her neck. He wanted to put his hand there, but they were gritty with mud. “The colt is fine. It will take a few days for him to wear off the mud and his fear.” He wiped his fingers together wanting to touch her body.

Something had happened while he was gone. He wondered if she had gone into the shed. What could she have found? “Are you all right? You look -- different.”

"You, my good man have secrets you don't share, so too, do I." Stepping around his easel, she braced her hands on her hips. "I'm fine. I'm just tired from running all that way in the sand and you --," she look at him from toe to head, "you need a shower." Flipping her hands, she shooed him out the door. "Go outside now to the shower, Buddo. I'll bring you a towel. Turn about fair play." A wicked grin spread across her face.

Lise brought him a towel after sweeping his muddy tracks of sand from the kitchen and porch. She sat on the porch "viewing stand," giving a hoot when he pulled off his shirt. "I'm getting turned on. I'm warning you," she hollered from her perch. "I should be angry at you, I found your cell phone, Mr. Secretive. But instead, some very naughty thoughts are seeping into my head."

His body hummed in anticipation. Grayson attempted to stay behind the shower curtain, but the wind played havoc on his cover. He unabashedly pulled the curtain back, showering in her full view.

"Do you think your grandparents did this when they were young?"

"Why not?" He rinsed off the suds. "I'd like to think they did." Not an ounce of shyness remained in the man as he took his time reaching for the towel.

SIXTEEN

At that moment, Casey began barking. Grayson's head snapped up to see a woman coming over the hill. "Oh great," he grumbled, 'bad timing seems to be my forte." His hands shook from the exertion of pulling the colt out of the mud. Grayson thought a jump in the bed might be a pleasant reward to revive his body and mood, but that wasn't going to happen with Josie coming down the hill. Wrapping a towel around his body, he threw his wet shorts and shirt over the clothesline.

He tucked the corner of the towel into the waist as Josie marched into the yard. Casey barked a few times but quieted when Lise grabbed his collar, hushing him.

"Well, isn't this cozy?" Josie emptied sand from her tiny shoe and brushed off a foot. "You've set up housekeeping. Hello, I'm Josie." She reached out a manicured hand.

"Lise," Grayson interrupted. "Her name is Lise and she's staying with me for a while." He climbed the steps.

"Excuse me, ladies, I seem to have lost my pants somewhere." He disappeared through the screen door.

"That was awkward," Josie eyed the young woman holding the dog, "but no harm done. It appears you have a positive effect on the man, if you know what I mean." She smirked as her eyebrow arched. Josie bent over and stared into Lise's face. "You can talk, can't you?"

"Yes." Lise rose to shake the woman's hand. Josie wore enough makeup to make a circus clown green with envy. "I'm -, we're -, oh hell. Would you like something to drink?" Lise looked at the black belt banding the bright yellow linen jacket over a pencil-thin black skirt. Strands of beads clung to the intruder's neck. "Not really dressed for a boat ride and running down sand dunes, are you?"

"He insists I come here. He never comes to town anymore and now I understand why." A full-pout lip pushed out as she gave Lise the once over. "I hired a boat to bring me here and, well, yes. If you don't mind, I'll take a glass of tea or anything stronger if you have it."

Grayson came out of the house carrying three glasses of tea. "I have nothing stronger. You know that. Have a seat. After hiking over the beach and hill you might like to sit a spell."

Josie sat rocking as she fanned her face and held the glass against her neck. "I don't see how you live out here. There's nothing to do. It appears you watch each other take showers for entertainment. Mosquitoes and no restaurants, no social-life, no…

"Interruptions," he finished for her. Grayson sat on the steps leaning back staring at his two guests. Lise, rocked slowly back and forth listening to the conversation. Her jealousy grew with each rock.

"Lise, Josie is here to see my new paintings and she'll set the tone for the show that's coming up in a couple of weeks. She sends out invitations, arranges catering, and drags money out of potential buyers. And for doing all that she gets a large percentage of my sales."

"You don't need much to live here. You said so yourself." Josie opened a small purse and reapplied her gloss over her lipstick. She snapped the compact closed and reached over and patted Lise's leg. "We've had this conversation before, you see. I'm humoring this talented, but crude man. *Humph*, he acts like selling paintings is something I can do while I'm having my nails done." She ran a hand atop her salon appointed curls and crossed her legs in his direction.

Grayson couldn't help but notice the black lace slip peeking out from under her skirt. His annoyance grew each time Josie eyed the two of them. He wished he could read Lise's mind when she shifted in her chair.

"I don't have all day. I want to get back to civilization as quickly as possible. What have you got to show me?" Josie's eyebrow went up suggestively as she mocked Lise. Standing up, the colorfully dressed woman brushed invisible lint from her front.

Holding the door open, he said, "After you." Josie entered.

"I'll stay out here and be out of your way." Lise drew one leg up on the chair and hugged her knee.

Josie studied the paintings that Grayson leaned against the walls of the small room. "She came about here, right?"

"Yes."

"Excellent, new subject matter and it's good. Very good." She pulled a small digital camera out of her purse and framed a shot. "Not a beautiful face, but captivating, don't you think?"

Josie was smart, not disapproving of Lise's features. He waited for her to say more. "She's…" He smudged a corner of a cloud with his thumb and stood back, his voice lowered. "She's captivating."

"Well, that's nice for you both. I'll be on my way and you two can play house some more. Is there a double feature today?" She patted his shoulder. "Just joking, my dear." She glimpsed through her camera files of the shots she had taken and then jerked her head in his direction. "You'll have all these delivered to the gallery by the Thursday before the opening, won't you?" She turned and looked out the window following his gaze to Lise. She was throwing a ball for the dog.

"Will she be at the show? There'll be an uproar if you bring the missing heiress, or should I say thief?" Her head cocked as she frowned.

"You recognized her?"

"Of course I recognized her. Her picture has been plastered in all the newspapers for the last week. What is going on here anyway?"

"She's lost her memory. She doesn't remember anything."

"Well, Erickson, if I shaved my head, lost thirty pounds and found someone who still let me climb aboard every night, I'd want to keep them in the dark, too!" She waggled a finger at him. "I won't say anything, but you can bet someone else will see her and notice. You could get arrested for harboring a fugitive."

"She's not a fugitive." He stared out the widow as he bit his lip. "Don't put any of the paintings with her pictures in the brochures unless I tell you." He placed his hand on her shoulder. "She didn't steal the money. It's been misplaced, that's all."

"Oh, so you believe that, do you? She manages millions and you don't think there's some off-shore bank holding those funds? Really, did that cancer eat out all the common sense in your brain as well?"

He felt his jaw tighten as he looked at the woman. "You and I have a business relationship. You don't want to break that relationship and lose any future income for brokering my work, do you?" He didn't wait for a response. "I think it's time you left."

"Your business is my business!" She grabbed up her purse and headed out the door.

When Lise turned to watch, Josie gave Grayson a kiss while rubbing her body, like a cat in heat, against Grayson's bare chest. Both of his hands tightened around her arms as he pushed her away.

Josie used her most suggestive voice, "Well, Love, I look forward to seeing you at the show." To Lise she smiled beautifully and said, "I guess I'll be seeing you again if you stick around." She turned and made her way across the yard. Her hips sashayed with every step. Her heels spiked tiny pits in the sand.

Both sets of eyes watched until she disappeared behind the dune that led to the dock. Grayson wiped his mouth, smudging the red lipstick in his palm. "I need to get back to the painting. Can you keep yourself busy?"

"I always keep myself busy for you." Jealousy screamed inside Lise's head and tightened every muscle in her neck and shoulders. "How about you open that shed and let me borrow your little four-wheel jalopy. I can handle it." She wanted to get away from the memory of that woman's mouth on his.

"Josie is not my lover, Lise. If you believe nothing else I have to say, believe that."

Lise said nothing and only stared back at him.

"She did that to make you jealous. Can't you see?" He crossed his arms over his chest. "No, you may not use the Mule. If you want to be gone, then go for another one of your long walks and don't go back to your brother's island." With that, he turned and slammed the screen door.

Lise looked at the dog, "He has temper tantrums, doesn't he? How do you live with him?" Casey merely jumped up on her and gave her a slobbering kiss. "*Ugh.*" She wiped her face. "So,ok, you've proved it's possible to get a kiss you don't want. Lesson learned, thank you very much, Casey. Come on dog." She headed over to the ocean side of the island.

SEVENTEEN

Lise walked down to the inlet. Both tide and wind were heading in the same direction making the water lay down. She noticed Ella's boat trawling in her direction. She waved releasing the tension that had climbed up on her shoulders during the visit. Ella wound in her line and eased her boat towards the shore. Lise waded out until her thighs were in the water and caught the bow of the vessel. "Want company?"

"Climb aboard. I 'magine you get bored, the way you're boxed up on that island." Ella pulled another cigarette from her pack. "This will keep the cough down, medicinal purposes only now." Ella placed the lighter back inside the cigarette package and pocketed them both. "I don't remember how old I was when I started. They killed my husband and they'll take me soon enough."

"I don't like you talking like that."

Ella shrugged and then handed Lise a fishing pole. "You've done this enough. Put it in the water and we'll catch us some dinner, tha-r."

Lise took the rod and caste off the stern. “Thanks. Glad to have another person to talk with,” Lise said. “He can be rather tiresome at times, can’t he?”

Ella maneuvered the boat out past the short waves of the surf and threw her line overboard, allowing the line to spin off the reel. “Been fishing with and without a man most of my life.” She smiled at the younger woman. “It’s better with.”

“You’ve always lived here?”

“No, we came from an island further north of here. Settled here in the ‘50s. I recon’ I’ll die here. I don’t worry about Pauli anymore. He’s good. He fends for himself now. Got his driver’s license and holds down a job, helps me with the store and he can make change.” She looked out over the stern of the boat as if talking to herself. “Guess that’s about all a body needs to learn in life.”

“I wish my life was that simple. It gets so complicated and I can’t remember the whole of it yet, only little things. Pieces come back.” She looked up. “You wouldn’t tell me more, would you?”

“Honey, he said you’d remember it all when you felt like it. You have mostly, haven’t you?”

“The more I relax, the more memories come back.”

“I sent you the newspapers. Didn’t they help?”

“Oh, I forgot about them. Grayson must have put them somewhere. I’ll look for them tonight.” She glanced toward the shore. The dog was laying on the beach keeping an eye on them. Lise ran her hand across her stomach. “I’m not pregnant.”

"*Humph*, too bad. You'd make a good mother."

"I figured since you got me the test, you deserved to know the results. I remembered I went to a fertility center. I decided to have a baby on my own using a sperm donor."

The older woman cackled. "Law' they have everything now at the store don't they." She leaned over and nudged Lise, "Between you and me, I prefer getting pregnant the old fashioned way." She grinned wide enough for Lise to see the gold in her bridgework. "I had a good man. He died twenty-eight years ago, but he's waiting for me." She nodded. "We talk every night. Now that Pauli's doing so well, I can go be with the man who made me a woman." She blew a stream of smoke out her nose and looked to the sky. Ella scratched her cheek with her thumb then took another drag on her cigarette.

"Don't say things like that. You can still fish and work, feed yourself, get around. I need you. Who else would I talk and fish with?"

"I think if I got so's I couldn't do for m'self, I'd rather die." She placed her hand on her chest.

"Well, don't die on me today. Promise me that." Lise tugged her rod back to check for a bite. "I want to fish and I haven't done this in a while. You stick around for me. Ok?"

"I'll do my best, honey. Besides I want to see how this all works out."

Lise eyebrows went up as she questioned the woman's remark.

"You know, between you and him." Ella lifted her chin towards the house and squinted, looking over the sand dunes. "I have an interest in that."

"Do you now?" Lise wound her line in all the way to find a small bluefish. She expertly unhooked its lip and tossed it back into the water. "I don't think anything will happen. There's an attraction all right, but we fight too much. It won't last. He can be so hard-headed at times."

"Yes, he can be that. Of course, you aren't the woman your mother was, thank goodness." She reached inside a small cooler and brought out a water jug. "My husband and I bickered all the time, but the making up was good. Want some?" She wiped out a tin cup and poured a cup for Lise. "I got an orange if you want some of that."

"Thanks, maybe later. Remember we need to catch dinner."

"Well, now that you mention it. With your help, we can set the net. Let's go around the inlet and drop her to the water. The tide's coming in and I bet we'll get a few." She smiled another wide grin and began reeling in her line. "Come steer the boat, honey, while I get things ready." She crouched low in the boat and crawled forward to unravel the float lines and anchor.

Lise felt at home at the wheel. She turned the boat and noticed the dog followed them along the shore.

"Go right up over the sand wedge," Ella pointed. "Cut your speed. Good. That's good. Now hold it." She dropped a small anchor and chain overboard to hold the fishing net in place. Attached to the bottom of the net, lead weights hit the side of the boat as the net tumbled into the water. "The current will take us down a ways."

"Let me do that. You take the wheel." Lise reached out for the pile of net, weights and cork line." Ella moved back to the stern of the boat and maneuvered the boat as Lise laid the net over the side. It had been stacked in the boat in a zigzag fashion the last time it was hauled aboard. Lise noticed the gray specks of dirt on the side of the boat where the net in the past had splattered the sandy mud. "Your Daddy built this boat and he fished in it teaching you, huh?"

"He brought the juniper down from the Albemarle Sound and we soaked it so's it would bend for that at the bow there. Our family fished for generations and building boats jest as long. This here boat was named for me, the *Ella Mae*." She rubbed her liver-spotted hand along the gunnels. "We never took the time to paint the name back on when we repainted her the last time. But she carries my name, the *Ella Mae*." She started coughing again and poured herself another cup of water. "Let's go ashore and sit a spell. My bones are aching. Must be a storm brewing out there." Her eyebrows narrowed as she scanned the horizon. "It'll be here within the week. I can feel it before the weatherman, with all his fancy instruments, makes the forecasts. There's a low a'coming for sure."

Lise dropped the other anchor, chain and float over the side of the boat and sat back on her seat while Ella steered the boat around the inlet and cut the engine as the skiff drifted into shore. Lise got out and tugged the boat closer, allowing Ella an easier step down.

The older woman rolled up her pants and dipped her canvas shoes into the water. “Still cool, ain’t it?” Once the boat was aground, Ella shifted her weight onto the gunnel and eased her body over the side. “Tide’s incoming. Lets pull her up closer or we’ll have to swim out to her later.”

Lise stepped on the anchor, wedging it deep in the sand and followed Ella up to the steep sand banks. Casey ran to them, looking like he was glad to have them ashore again.

Ella found a shelf in the sand ridge and leaned her back against the sun-warmed sand. “I read an article about someone who filled a sock with sand and heated it in a microwave oven. Now where you think he got that idea? Probably like this. He scooted himself into the sand one day and came on to the idea.” She nested her bottom and back burrowing her shoulders further into the warmth. “Now he makes thousands of dollars selling sand-filled socks as neck and back warmers.” Gleefully she added, “Now don’t that beat all?” Within minutes, she dozed on her sandy bench, the straw hat shading her face.

Lise took note and found her own shelf, wedging herself into a sandy resting place. Casey put his head at her feet. The winds shifted and sea oats scored arcs in the sand nearby. She dozed as the tide rose.

In her dream, Lise was fishing with Teddy, aboard their father’s boat. Those laughing gulls were everywhere. Like children playing king of the hill, they soared and settled on pilings along the waterway as Teddy guided the boat into the inlet. The old mahogany wood run-about rocked her gently while the sun cooked her skin. After a while, Teddy tossed down his rod, balanced on the bow, a foot on each side of the bowsprit, then back-flipped into the water. A pre-teen Lise jumped up and scooted to see where he went. Teddy swam around the boat, splashing water up on her, while she shouted outrageous threats back. She picked up the bailer and tossed water at him to even the score.

"Come on in. The water's fine," he urged her.

She tossed out the anchor, knowing she should have lowered it carefully.

"Hey, you know better," he charged. "You're supposed to let it go easy over the side you, dingbat! The line'll tangle into a mess if you're not careful."

"I'm not a dingbat." She puckered her lips and scowled at him. "It's down ain't it? It'll grab. How deep you think it is?"

"Here, it should be about twenty feet." He swished her again with a handful of saltwater.

She tasted the salt on her lip as she squirmed out of the clothes she wore over her swimsuit. "You're not afraid of sharks or jelly fish?"

"Nope, come on in."

They'd done this many times before so she was used to diving off the boat. The cold shocked her, but as she paddled around, her body warmed. She selfishly enjoyed these boating trips, but still had fears of the water, like all twelve-year-olds. Most of her friend's brothers were closer in age, but Teddy was a full grown man now with a job working with their daddy. He promised to take her fishing on his next trip down to the coast. A month into her summer vacation, Lise was bored. She moped around the house until Teddy arrived, but then talked her mother into letting them go out in the boat that same afternoon.

"The only monster you have to worry about, Annie, is me!" He dove down under her, grabbing her toes.

She squealed in delight and took a deep breath to follow him under the water. The salt burned her eyes as she searched for him.

"Hey, dummy, you tangled the anchor line," he called at her from the bow.

"*Huh*, who you calling a dummy?" She swam to the front of the boat where he was treading water. He dove beneath the water again and then came up shooting a fountain of saltwater above his face as he floated on his back.

Annie punched him down and climbed on his shoulders to jump off. "Race you around the boat!" She dove into the water and swam toward the stern. When she couldn't see or hear him, she thought he dived and was porpoising under the boat -- cheating on her again. She scooted underwater, mermaiding her way back to the front of the boat. She still couldn't find him so she glided to the surface to grab another mouth of air. "Teddy, where are you?" She swam around the boat to the other side. "Teddy!"

The icy silent water yanked the fun out of her. "Where are you?" Now she was angry. She dove down, this time under the boat. The murky water filtered tiny sea particles like dandruff falling from the keel to the sandy bottom below. She came up on the other side of the boat once more. Her young body shivered. Her teeth chattered as the cold water increased her fear.

"Teddy Basnight, this is no fair. You're scaring me. Please come here, now." Her throat scratched as she coughed out salt water. "Are you back up in the boat? You are going to be so sorry when I get you." She swam to the stern of the boat, pushed her toe up on the step and grabbed the transom. Her wet foot slipped. "Ouch, that hurts!" She dropped back into the water. She lunged again, pulling herself aboard.

"No. No. No." Lise woke with a scream.

Ella jerked her head and sat up. "What's wrong, honey." She pulled herself up and stooped down next to Lise. "You have a bad dream?"

"No, Ella. Yes, I remembered." She still tasted the saltwater burning in her throat as she remembered that day. "I'm Annie, I mean Anne Basnight, but it was you who found his body and pulled it out. He was tangled in the anchor line. I didn't know until I heard them talking about it weeks later. I hid under the piano in the living room and listened as the Coast Guardsmen explained to my parents. My brother probably tried to loosen the loop in the line and was caught in the rode. The weight of the anchor pulled him down. It was an accident." She grabbed the woman's arms. "I didn't kill him. It wasn't my fault. Tell me it was an accident."

"Yes, child, we never blamed you. Your daddy took it bad and your mother, well, your mother was your mother." She hugged Lise to her chest.

Ella smelled of tobacco, fish and lilac bath powder. That squeeze and odor opened another door to her mind. Ella Armstrong had held her the same way the day Teddy died. Eric and Pauli had pulled his body aboard their boat, while their mother had held her. They were brothers! Ella was their mother. Lise remembered Eric Armstrong. He was Grayson or Minnow, her lover of the past week.

EIGHTEEN

"You all right now, honey?" Ella brushed Lise's hair out of her face. You remembered about your pesky brother. That's good. I mean, it's good you remembered that all." Ella slowly stood up, one hand on her back.

"Pesky brother? I idolized him, didn't I?"

"No child. Maybe you wished that, but you cringed when he came around. He bullied my boys, pulled the wool over your parents' eyes. I don't think he was evil, just not brought up right. Your daddy let him get away with too much." She patted Lise on the back as she held her. "But let's not talk bad of the dead."

"I didn't like him? He teased Pauli and Eric. Yes, I remember that now." She stood up, holding Ella's arm.

"I didn't like him, but I didn't kill him." She rubbed her arm. "I admit I wished he was dead a time or two after he pulled some mean trick on me. I guess that bothered me. I felt like his death was my fault. I had to pay Daddy back for killing his son."

"Well, girl, that's not the way it was."

"But Daddy said I killed him and never forgave me." Lise reached to wipe tears from her eyes.

"Well he shouldn't have done that. You were a little girl and your brother was a man who should have knowed better." Ella voice rose until another coughing fit took away her breath.

Lise grabbed the water bottle and held it for the woman while she sipped a bit down.

"Thank you, sweetheart. Here now, we need to be getting back to our net. Don't want the crabs to be eating our supper." She brushed the sand from her backside and followed the younger woman out towards the boat.

Lise asked, "The man I call Grayson is your Mr. Armstrong. Both he and Pauli are your sons, aren't they?"

"True, I'm proud to say that." She coughed again. "Lord, come get me now. I can hardly get my breath."

"Don't talk like that."

"If you only knew how much I'd like to see you two together. I see it might work. If I go, I'll be watching you when I'm up there." She turned her head upward.

Lise felt her face warm at the woman's comments. "If we are going to be together he hasn't mentioned it to me. But you call him - Eric, Mr. Armstrong?" She felt like she was in a dark house with lights blinking in the rooms. Flashes of memory flickered in her mind. "You never did when he was a boy."

"His daddy was living then. I always called his daddy, Mr. Armstrong. When his daddy died, Eric told me to call him Mr. Armstrong and he'd take care of me like his daddy did." She nodded her head. "He has, took care of us both, me and Pauli for years now." She waded into the water and picked up the anchor. "Pauli may be slow, but he's smart, too. I'm looking forward to seeing my old man again. You s'pose he'll recognize this old wrinkled woman?"

"Hush!" Lise stood in front of the woman. "I just remembered about my brother's death and here you say you want to die! Stop talking like that. Remember, you want to see how it ends with Grayson and me. I mean Eric, your Mr. Armstrong." Lise placed both fists at her waist, notching her body just above her belt line. "Now, let's go haul in those fish." She towed the boat closer into shore where the older woman could climb aboard easier. Lise lifted the big dog up and helped him climb aboard, too.

Her sandals squished in the boat as Lise moved back and forth hauling in the net. Ella tugged the fish free and tossed the small ones back into the water. By the time the net was entirely aboard and layered for its next use, the sky was pink.

"Stay and have supper with us." Lise invited her. They had docked. Ella blew the horn for Grayson to come.

"No, no. Pauli will be worried. I imagine you both will have a lot to talk about." Ella pointed at her son coming down to the beach. "A lot to talk about." She repeated herself as her son drew near. "Y'all have a good evening now. It's gonna be a real pretty sunset in a little bit. Nice day tomorrow by that sky." With that, she pulled into the sound once more.

"We caught fish." Lise held up the plastic grocery bag of fish. Lise grabbed Grayson's arm. "Eric."

He froze, waiting for what came next.

"We need to talk. I remembered almost everything now. Your family had a store at the boat ramp. We bought bait and off-loaded our boat. That was before we had the dock with boat lifts. My name is Anne. You used to call me Annie and Peanut."

They had reached the house and Eric started cleaning the fish.

"Shall I make us some tea?"

"No."

"We need to talk. Teddy was horrible and you let me think he was my hero. Why?" Her mind couldn't seem to keep up with her mouth. "Do you want me to call you Eric again?"

"I was getting used to our names. If you don't mind we'll keep them until you leave."

"To make a long story short, I know about my past and our families. Daddy didn't want us to be around you much, but Teddy never did what Daddy told him and I just tagged along."

Grayson nodded.

"You must have thought I was a real twerp. Spying and following you around all the time."

Grayson took her hand and squeezed it. "I enjoyed the attention. You were a cute little thing. You've grown into a beautiful woman, but I miss the long pigtails." He tugged the back of her hair and grinned.

“You may as well bring in your cell phone and wallet. I saw them when you went to rescue the colt, but I didn’t look to see your name. You sneak, calling Ella and telling her to bring stuff. I should be angry at you.” She beat her fist on the table three times. “If I think about it any longer, I’ll get angry at you -- all your psycho-analyzing me and me cringing every time I tried to remember.”

“But you did remember. I didn’t have to fill any of it in for you.”

“It was painful.”

“Are you pregnant?”

“No. What do you care?” She pulled her hands back and sat up in the chair, sad he hadn’t talked about a future together. “I have to leave so I can clear myself. As soon as I remember this last piece, I have to leave.”

NINETEEN

"I *think* I know about the money thing." The next morning, Lise sat with a book, legs crossed Indian style on the couch. It had rained early in the morning. The smell of rain still lingered in the air. "Grayson, I need to go back to fix it."

"They'll arrest you and I'll never see you again."

She smirked, "You can come to my trial."

"It's not funny. There's a lot of money at stake. They think you took it."

"I'm going home."

She watched him as his jaw moved back and forth. He threw a brush down on his stand. *Why doesn't he ask me to come back after it's all over?* She crossed her fingers and hoped he'd say the three words she wanted to hear.

"I'll call Pauli."

"Beeeep! Wrong response." Lise felt disappointed that he wouldn't tell her his feelings, but she wasn't going to beg.

"What?"

He has no clue! Perhaps the past week she was merely playing on her childhood infatuation with him. Maybe she didn't love him and for sure, he didn't love her. He took advantage of the situation. She pouted thinking maybe Josie and he had a thing going after all.

"Don't be like this." He leaned over her, an arm on each side of her head and kissed her forehead.

"Don't tell me how to be. You had almost two weeks to tell me things, but you didn't. You played doctor with me -- in more ways than one." She pushed him away, tiring of his game.

"Is this what you want?" His mouth gaped in confusion. "What have I done to upset you now?" He almost knocked his jar of brushes over as he spread his arms in exasperation.

"Ask Pauli if he can pick me up early."

He walked into the kitchen and grabbed the cell phone off the kitchen countertop. "Ask him yourself." He tossed it to her.

Lise caught the phone, turned it on and dialed the number stored in memory. An excited Pauli answered. "I've been calling you! Mama's gone. She went to Daddy."

"Calm down Pauli. Now tell me everything."

Grayson jerked his head around when he heard Lise's change of tone. "Wait, you need to tell this to your brother."

***

A low moved into the area and a storm lashed the coast, delaying Ella's memorial service. For three days, the winds of a northeaster bashed their shoreline making it impossible to get off island. Lise calmed her emotions during the difficult time for Grayson's benefit. When the weather cleared, Lise followed Grayson out to his larger boat, now tied to the dock. "I want to go with you. We've known you were going to town for the funeral for the past three days and I've decided I want to be there."

"Someone will recognize you and put two and two together. They'll remember Ted's house. Do you want to be recognized or arrested?"

"What difference will it make? I was going back home to Charlotte, anyway a few days ago. Grayson, Ella was my friend, too!"

"Whatever." Grayson shrugged and untied the lines. They had pulled the larger boat out of its winter shelter and tied it to the dock during a calm. Lise jumped aboard and pushed the boat away from the dock.

"I'll change at my family's home on the waterway. Just let me off at the dock. When I'm through dressing up in Mama's clothes, even you'll have a hard time recognizing me." She took a seat inside the cabin and waited for him to increase speed. The thrum of the big engine told her the boat had reached cruising speed and was planing on top of the water. Within the hour, she jumped off his boat onto her family dock and made her way up to the big familiar house.

Once more, she found the key under the flowerpot, opened the door and went straight to her mother's closet. She pulled clothes out trying to decide. *Which will be more appropriate and the best disguise? The navy pantsuit and wide brimmed hat might work.* She turned on the shower and stripped off her clothes.

***

At the funeral home, local friends and customers from years of buying tackle and boating supplies crowded into the foyer. A steady line of acquaintances passed Ella's two surviving sons. Grayson turned and adjusted Pauli's tie. "You ok?"

Pauli nodded his head. "I'm ok. You ok?" He mimicked his older brother, patting his brother's back. "Mama's with Daddy, so we should be glad."

"Good attitude, bro." Grayson's breath caught in his throat when he looked at the next woman in line.

"How are you Mr. Armstrong? I'm so sorry to hear of your mother's death." Behind dark glasses and a wide brim hat, Lise could feel his eyes focusing on her. "Pauli, are you running the store now?"

The older man nodded, but then realized who was speaking to him. Grayson nudged his arm to remind him of their secret. "Yes, m'am. Business as usual tomorrow. Will your husband be fishing any time soon? I'll tell him the best spots to go."

Lise held Pauli's hand in both of hers. "You do that, Pauli. I'll tell him." Pauli giggled at their secret, and then reached to greet the next person in the line.

Lise sat near the back of the church, close to the door. She kept her head down for most of the service, thankful for the glasses and hat that hid her face. She glanced up once feeling Grayson's stare. When she did, she caught the eye of another man who was standing near the door. She looked away and as soon as the benediction ended the service, she shifted out of the pew and strode away from the church. She paced down the street feeling a set of eyes drilling into her spine.

Lise window-shopped along the quiet street, catching her reflection in the window. She hadn't spent a lot of time the past month looking at her face. She was shocked at seeing her mirror image. A movement reflected in the window of a figure across the street. The unknown man was still tailing her.

She entered her second antique store for the day and hurried to the back. Having been a seasonal resident of the town for years, she knew where the rear entrance and alley led and ducked through the park hedge, losing her stalker. After making her way back to the family house without further problems, Lise changed back into her island clothes. She found a scarf, tied her red hair up and then plopped a new hat on her head followed by the sunglasses. She couldn't chance waiting for Grayson at his family home, so she strolled back along the waterfront and climbed aboard his boat. She curled herself into a ball in the cuddy cabin and waited.

Hours later, she felt someone step aboard the boat. "Don't move an inch. Someone's watching." Grayson spoke under his breath as he started the engine. He had changed back into casual clothes before leaving town.

He let the diesel engine warm up and then he loosened the lines and drifted out into the waterway. “Stay down there. He’s walked out on the dock.” Grayson lifted his hand to wave to the sharp-eyed stranger and turned the boat in the direction of the inlet. “Have you been hiding all afternoon?”

Without moving she responded, “He followed me from the funeral. You were right. I created a problem for you. I’ll leave tomorrow.” She waited again, hoping for the any words to invite her to stay or comeback when she cleared herself.

Arriving back on the Island, Lise helped tie the boat to the dock. Grayson put his arm around her back. The warmth of his arm comforted her. Together they walked to the house.

“Are you hungry?” He looked in the refrigerator. “I ate at Pauli’s. Neighbors brought in casseroles, cakes, and everything you can imagine. Lots of church ladies are looking after him.”

He chuckled. “He has enough food to last him a month or more.”

“Does Pauli have a girlfriend?”

Grayson felt the hairs on the back of his neck prickle. “That’s an odd question to ask here -- now.” He had always been around to defend his brother in the past if needed. Was she prying into his life again?

She shrugged, "Well, he is an attractive man and he has a good job. I'm interested in your family."

"Well it's none of your business. I mean, I don't know. We never talk about - that. Did you say you were hungry?"

"I'll make a sandwich." She pulled eggs and bread from the refrigerator. She fried two eggs and piled them onto the whole wheat bread with lettuce and tomato. They sat down to eat, but Casey began barking. Grayson looked out of the door to see a man in a brown uniform come over the sand dune from the dockside of the island.

"Go upstairs and stay out of sight." He pulled her plate over to his side of the table, sat back down and waited. He felt the heavy boots hit the porch before he heard the voice.

"Eric, you here?" The sheriff's deputy peered through the screen door.

"Come on in, Sam." Having grown up in the same town, Grayson recognized the man from his former high school. "I was just eating. Can I fix you anything?"

"No, no. Sorry to hear about your mama." The man gave him a puzzled look and sat down in Lise's recently vacated chair. "There's a reporter in town who thinks you're hiding Anne Basnight out here on your island. Know anything about that?" His face revealed nothing to his former football team member.

"Who?' Grayson faked a frown. "Annie Basnight that scrawny little girl who used to run around town." He wondered if Lise could hear his description from wherever she was hiding.

"She's a grown woman now and from the pictures on the television, a real looker. Her folks used to vacation down here. I guess they came to your family's store a lot. You haven't seen her here or over on the other island have you?"

Grayson shook his head. "Can't say I've seen an Anne Basnight around here lately."

"She's in some trouble over in Charlotte. I called the detective over there and they haven't found her yet. He wants her for questioning. You didn't hear about all the money she took?"

"I stay on the island, Sam. Don't get a paper. I have no television."

Casey came up to the officer and sniffed his leg. Sam reached down and patted the dog.

"Mind if I look around?"

"You have a search warrant?"

"I guess I could get one, but I'm only doing my job, Eric. Give me a break."

Grayson finished the sandwich and washed his hands in the sink. He let the dog outside and said, "No, I don't care. There's not much here. What you see is pretty much all there is."

"How about upstairs, I need to look."

"No problem. I want to get back to my painting. I have a show in a couple of weeks. Would you and your wife like to come? I'll send you some tickets." He followed the other man upstairs.

The deputy gave a low whistle. "Nice what you did to this old house. If my wife saw this, she'd want to tear out some walls and paint our bedroom this color." He tapped the walls as he looked out on the deck and then peered into the bathroom. He hesitated, about to pull the shower curtain aside when the dog started barking again. Both men crowded together at the bathroom window to look out. Another person had come over the rise and was stumbling down the sandy dune.

"Is that your reporter fellow?" Grayson asked.

"*Uh-huh.*"

"*Hmm*, can you do me a favor, Sam?" He turned and led the way down the steps again. "Would you go out there and tell him this is a private island and I don't care for people here, unless they're invited." He opened the door for his old friend. "After you do that, I'll show you into all the other buildings, if you want."

"Sounds like a plan, my friend." The deputy adjusted his gun belt and then walked out to speak with the intruder. Grayson stood back from the door and watched.

***

A short while later he walked the deputy down to the dock. The tan and gray johnboat with center console bobbed in the water. "I appreciate your concern, Sam. I've been a loner out here for several months now. Mama brought me supplies, but now Pauli can do it, as he has time. I'll keep a look out for this Annie Basnight. Sorry, I was no help to you."

"Oh, I think she'll show up." He tipped his hat and started the engine. "Good to see you again. You licked that cancer. You're looking a lot better than the last time I saw you."

"I hope so. I'm feeling better. That Annie Basnight should turn up probably within the week."

"That's good to know." The deputy looked him in the eyes. "I'm counting on it."

"You take care," Relieved, Grayson untied and shoved the boat off the dock.

The police officer reversed the marine patrol boat and then headed for the nearby channel.

Grayson sauntered back over to his house and walked upstairs. He swished back the shower curtain to find Lise huddled in the tub, her towel and wash cloth in hand. "Found you."

"She held up the towel and said, "Barely had time to remove the evidence before you were up here. Was he being nice or is he really dumb?"

"Guess he was being nice. When he walked in the living room, he was surrounded by my paintings. Any fool would have recognized you."

She grinned. "Guess it's nice to have friends in high places."

He leaned his forehead against hers for a moment. "It's good to have friends."

"Friends." She wished again he'd say more, but he didn't.

"I'm tired." He lay down on the bed and put his head back. "All I wanted to do today was bury my mother without people going crazy and showing up to look for the missing heiress who stole some company's retirement monies."

"Oh, so now I'm only your missing thief-heiress?" She took offense.

"Don't be like this. I'm under a lot of stress here. I apologize if I offended you."

"I need to leave this island. It's too - too boring."

He rolled over and looked at her. She wore the clothes he paid for. She had a deep tan and natural highlights in her hair from her stay. Her moods were beginning to shift back and forth again, like the sands outside his door. She hadn't indicated that she wanted to come back or if she had any feelings for him. "So, you're leaving, for good."

She nodded. "I'll call Pauli. Don't get up." She went down the steps but returned a moment later. "Grayson, did you say missing retirement funds?" His only response was a soft snore.

***

"He can't come until tomorrow. He said he already scheduled some yard work for a lady." She looked up at him the next morning after his walk. "Pauli is a very determined man."

"Don't make fun of him."

"I'm not." She stared up at him with a question on her face, but she still didn't say anything.

"Did you remember any more since the last time we caught up?" It was over a month that they had been living on his island.

"Yes, you said retirement money."

"The entire retirement fund of some company in Charlotte is missing, almost a million dollars. Any bells going off?"

"I bet they made a real sob story on that about all the people who have no retirement and it's my fault."

"As a matter of fact, they did. Police investigations focused on you and the funds disappearing about the same time." Grayson turned back to his painting as he filled in a color while he listened to her.

She propped her head on a cushion and was lying across the couch with her book. "My job is to handle the large accounts at the firm. Once a corporation decides to invest their corporate funds, the money comes through my office. I set up the accounts and distribute the money in our various investment funds. The checks should be made out to our firm in care of their 401K or whatever retirement account they open." She looked up. He was making those irritating circular motions with his brush to hurry her story along.

"I remember getting a cashiers check made out to me. A cashier's check is the same as cash! That's not supposed to happen. And besides that, it supposed to be made out to our company trust account. I gave it back to Millie, my assistant, and told her to take care of it. We have a folder on each potential account. I bet that's the missing money. The amount of the check was a big one."

"If that's the case, how come she hasn't said anything all this time?"

"That, I don't know, but when I go back, I bet I can resolve this all very easily." She unfolded her legs for the couch and headed towards the kitchen. "Want anything to drink?"

"Tea would be lovely."

"I need to get back to my life and leave you to yours. With me gone you'd be able to paint all you want." She could feel the heat rise in her cheeks. "That's what you want, isn't it?" She placed his glass on the table and stood by the window. "I was just a convenience or an inconvenience whichever you needed - sex or painting." The words tasted bitter in her mouth.

"Why are you doing this?"

Lise couldn't make herself apologize or take the words back. Grayson wasn't asking her to stay. He'd never mentioned love. She became madder the longer he stood there staring at her, without a word. She could see the vein standing out on his temple. Splotches of red appeared around his healing scars.

"How could you throw out words like that to me? I thought you enjoyed what happened here between us."

"Us? What went on here…?" She searched her mind for the last time for his sake. "What went on here was that I lost my memory. We did a little canoodling to pass the time. I heard no complaints from your side of the bed, Eric Armstrong."

"Now you've overstepped your welcome. Was this all pity passion on your part?" He threw his brush down. "Are you saying that it was -- canoodling?" He pulled her up from the couch encircling both her arms with his hands. "You really mean what you're saying. I was a mere convenience to your horniness?"

She stared back at him, afraid to say anything.

"Well, the truth finally surfaces, does it? You've made me into a fool and no one gets the opportunity to do that again."

"Fine with me. You kept me here long enough and allowed me to think you were Teddy's friend, but all you wanted to do was – to get close to me. You hate me as much as you hated my brother."

"I loathed your brother," he snarled. He finally said it. "If you remember nothing else, remember how I hated him."

"You're disgusting. Vile." With that, she turned and ran outside.

Casey, who had cringed in the corner ever since their voices changed, let out a whine.

Grayson reached for his cell phone. "Pauli, I'm making sure you don't forget about tomorrow morning and picking up Lise for me. What time do you think you'll be here?"

"I can come tomorrow. I'll be there before breakfast, need to be back to open the store." His eagerness to please carried across the water.

"Sure, come before breakfast and see that she gets back to her car or car rental place, whatever, will you?" He still cared about her welfare, but he wouldn't admit it to her.

"Sure, boss. Pick her up, take her back and find a car. I can do it."

"I'm counting on you, pal. Thanks. Oh, I may not see you in the morning, but I appreciate this. I have to start boxing up my paintings and getting them ready to take to the gallery. Could you come back and help me with that tomorrow night? I'll fix us something for supper." He enjoyed talking to his brother man-to-man.

"Sure, boss." The older man hung up.

She heard the one-side conversation as she rocked in the porch chair. She was leaving the island and Grayson tomorrow. Her heart ached, but she couldn't say the words asking him for forgiveness. Why was he so -- so, intolerable? She had tried to monitor her frame of mind and gauge his moods. She couldn't see any reason for this all to explode between them. She had worked out her life's puzzle while being on his island. He wanted her to do that. They had fallen in love, hadn't they? *Why is love so hard? He can't know I've fallen in love with him. He doesn't want me here.*

The long evening finally brought night and for the last time they slept in the bed together, but apart. She wanted to reach across to him, confide her true feelings. Lise felt like she had only slept a few minutes when she opened her eyes to sunlight pouring in the room from the skylight. She quickly showered and dressed. Breakfast cereal and her tea bag sat at her place on the wooden table. She didn't feel like eating. She used her toothbrush one last time before she walked down to the dock. Grayson and the dog were nowhere in sight when Pauli arrived.

Lise took one final look toward the house. Her eyes found neither man nor dog. "Good. It's better this way."

Pauli leaned toward her after she spoke. "Miss Lise, what did you say?"

"I said it's good to be going home. I've missed it. I'm happy to finally get off this island." A familiar knot began to form in her stomach. She would return to her mother and her position at the investment firm.

Pauli might be slow, but he knew the words coming from Lise's mouth didn't match the look on her face. He carried Lise to the mainland and then delivered her to her car, after a brief stop at her waterfront home. She promptly started her car, waved goodbye and left.

TWENTY

"And who are you?" Anne walked up to her assistant's desk and spoke to the bleach-bottle blond. Surprised, the middle-aged woman knocked over her pen set. She rolled back from her desk and looked up. A straight row of paper clips and pencils in her open drawer hinted at the woman's personality. "I'm sorry, who are you?" The gold bracelet loaded with charms jangled from her wrist. Her cleavage exposing blouse was tucked tightly into the narrow band of skirt and her legs were cloaked in dark stockings. Lise bet that there was a panty girdle holding them up.

"Where's Millie?" After driving the five hours to Charlotte, Anne was in no mood to face a new underling. She'd only been gone a month. Why did things look differently? "Who placed that giant ficus tree by my office door?" She felt like she was entering a jungle, not her office. "I don't like it."

The blond couldn't find her tongue, but someone else spoke. "Anne, we've been worried sick. How are you?" Her mother and the branch manager, Dave Prescott came out of his office.

"Who put that tree there? I want it gone."

"Sweetheart," her mother leaned in for an air kiss, "I told them you had amnesia. I got that right, didn't I? I called the nice police detective who came to talk with me about all this trouble and there was a securities man who left his card. That was the right thing to do, wasn't it, dear?" Her mother's well-manicured hand went to her shellacked coiffure. She adjusted her jacket over her skirt. "Oh, dear, the reporters are here, too." Mrs. Basnight straightened her pearls and prepared to have her picture taken as a photojournalist appeared in the hallway. She grabbed her daughter, hugging Anne to her side. "Smile, dear. You want to look good in the paper." Under her breath, her mother whispered, "Nice outfit, Annie. You look smashing."

Anne recognized the reporter as the man who followed her from Ella's funeral service. Assuming her role as Vice President of Corporate Accounts, she addressed the small crowd that gathered. "Mother, detective, gentlemen, come into my office." She hesitated. "It is still my office, isn't it?"

When no one challenged her, she looked at her new assistant's name placard. "Ilea-Jean is it? Please get me the Blanchard Corporation file and all my new accounts files that I set up before my vacation. They are listed in the computer by date of last report."

Ilea-Jean looked for the manager's approval and then stood up to search the files as directed. The office manager's face colored as his hand went up to straighten his tie.

Within minutes, all sat in the office. Anne didn't feel very hospitable so she didn't ask Ilea-Jean for coffee. She looked from one face to the other. Her mother smiled demurely, sitting on the front edge of her chair, ready to escape out of the office as soon as possible. Dave Prescott crossed his legs in one armchair and frowned.

He looks disappointed. Maybe he hoped for a promotion with me missing. Now that I'm back in the office, I'll never trust the man again. He should have looked for the missing check with more enthusiasm.

The reporter gave her a polite smile and waited pencil poised to catch a quote. Her assistant reached over and brushed dandruff from Prescott's shoulder. Not missing the subtlety of the motion, Anne found what she was looking for among the file folders.

"Is this the check or missing money that you couldn't find?" She handed the cashier's check across to the police detective. "Attached is my note to Millie, my then assistant," she gave a meaningful look to both her manager and new assistant, "to call and explain the problem. She was to take care of the matter and then deposit a new check, made out correctly into their new accounts." With her sunburned face and new freckles, Anne struggled to maintain her official posture.

While she waited for someone else to say something, she briefly went over the previous six hours in her mind. She borrowed a pair of slacks and top from her mother's closet. She used Pauli's cell phone to call her mother, after she found her waterlogged Blackberry in the dishwasher. On reaching Charlotte, Anne stopped at her favorite boutique to buy new clothes, which delighted the boutique owner.

Her new black tuxedo collared sheath gave her dress for success a new kick. Her ankles were getting used to the heel height of her new open-toed sandals.

When no one said anything, she asked, “Where is Millie?” Anne looked around. “I was on vacation and didn’t know there was a problem. My Blackberry got wet and it didn’t work, and Mother, the phone is out of order at the house. How did that happen?”

Her mother shook her head. “I don’t know sweetheart, but we’ll have Gerald look into it.” She looked over at the reporter and detective. “Gerald is our handy-man in Southport, you see. He takes care of the house and the boat when we aren’t there.”

Anne continued her address. “I didn’t want to be disturbed. I told Millie I was taking a few days off. I was looking over a new business proposal from a competitor and it took my full attention. Then I had an accident and lost my memories of here and family. It took me a while to remember everything, but not to worry.”

She looked at the faces of the small audience before her. “I’ve regained all my memory and a better understanding of my priorities. Does anyone have other questions?” That satisfying all present, she dismissed them except for Ilea-Jean.

“You are never, ever, to question my instructions like you did a few minutes ago. Prescott does not own this firm.

Prescott's family did not spend sixty years building this institution. I am your boss unless I see fit to remove you. Is that clear?"

The woman in the two-piece navy suit with camisole peeking out gasped. "I'm so sorry. I didn't know who you were. Please forgive me. Millie quit and if I may share a bit of information, she ran off with a married man. She --"

"I don't care." Anne cut her off. "This is not a gossip mill and I'm sure she had her reasons. You or someone filed these folders without looking inside. If you make the same mistake again, you'll be filing for unemployment. Do I make myself clear?"

"Yes, ma'm, I apologize again." Ilea-Jean backed out of the office nearly stepping out of her shoes.

No sooner had the door closed behind the assistant than Anne rushed to her private bathroom. "Not again!" She vomited her late breakfast into the toilet and then looked at herself in the mirror while she wiped a damp paper towel across her mouth and forehead. She waited for the second heave which never came.

It was the first time in six weeks she had a chance to study her face with makeup on now. Sun streaks highlighted her hair and her freckles had popped out along her nose. Her eyes were too close together and her narrow nose was all wrong. Her mother often reminded her that she needed to use more makeup to hide those flaws. *Grayson thought my face was beautiful, but I need a haircut.* Anne looked at her unpainted fingernails. *Maybe I have time for a manicure but*

I'll let my toenails go for a while. A faint smile sprang to her face, and then melted away.

She walked back to her desk and reached for her rolodex. Picking up the phone, she punched in her private line and a telephone number. "Is Dr. Ward available? I need to see her as soon as possible." Anne looked at the bottles of pills in her attaché. "I went off my drugs and I need to talk to the doctor about starting them again."

"I'm sorry, but the earliest I can schedule you will be next month. If it's an emergency, you can come to the day clinic."

Anne sighed, "No, it's nothing I can't live with for another month." She made a note on her desk calendar.

***

A month later, Anne found herself in her doctor's office, bouncing her crossed leg impatiently as she waited for the doctor to return with the lab results.

A moment later, she heard a tap at the door. The physician eased into the room and sat at the desk. Her thick red hair fell from a banana clip. The green scrubs, rumpled from a full day's workload reminded Anne of deep green seawater. "You have been busy these past few months. Congratulations, you're pregnant! However, it wasn't my doing. You did this all by yourself or rather with a consenting male, I'm thinking." The doctor smiled and her eyebrow went up questioning her patient. "My little guys would be much bigger and the baby would be about five months along. Your baby is smaller. I'd say between two and three months?"

Anne counted back on her fingers. The helpful doctor handed her a calendar and together they nailed the probable time of conception. It was the first week on Grayson's island, perhaps the first time they made love.

The child was Eric's, but Anne hadn't heard from him since she left his island. "The father didn't want me and he certainly wouldn't want this child." She bit her lips to keep back her tears. "Would you have a problem if we said it was donated sperm? We can proceed as if I did this on my own, with your help of course."

"We'll do whatever you want, patient's confidentiality and all that is standard procedure. Are you sure you want to keep this from him? With you stopping the meds so suddenly, your hormones must have created a roller coaster ride with your emotions. You also mentioned your head being knocked and losing your memory. I don't see any permanent damage, except to this relationship."

Anne shook her head. "No, I don't think I'll ever see him again."

"Maybe you misjudged him. You said he was under a lot of stress when you parted. Don't you want to rethink it?" Her kind eyes were very perceptive.

"No. I'll let it be known that this is another success at your capable hands, the best fertility specialist in town." She pressed her lips together and nodded. "I'm certain."

When Anne returned home that night, her mother was sitting in the formal living room reading another one of her romance paperbacks. Her glasses were perched on the tip of her nose; her bare feet propped on the divan. Her long rose-colored silk caftan hung to the floor.

Anne smiled. “Mother, I never knew you polished your toenails.”

“There are probably a lot of things we don’t know about each other. Oh, my dear sweet girl, we’ve each played such a role. Your father directed the whole scene, even from his grave. We did as we were told like good Basnight women.” She closed her book and pulled off her glasses with both hands. Then she folded them in her lap.

Rubbing the bridge of her nose she said, “I missed you. It got me thinking. He’s been dead a long time and we still live in his shadow, don’t we?” Josephine Basnight’s eyebrows went up. “Don’t you think it’s time we lived our own lives?” She reached out her hand and pulled her daughter to her until they both curled into the corner of the massive couch.

Looking into the distance her mother said, “I’ve been thinking about who I want to be when I grow up. I’d like to take some ceramic classes at the community college. Did you know my mother was an artist? Your father pooh-poohed her. I bet you have an artistic bent in you also.”

“Trust me. Mother, I know I can’t paint. Maybe, I’ll try something else another time. I have to clear my plate before I can look for a hobby.”

Her mother patted her shoulder and ran her hand across Anne’s back.

"We used to do this when I was little, didn't we?" Anne took her mother's arm and clasped her fingers between those of her mother's. "You used to read to me here. Why did you stop?"

"Your father thought we should quit babying you. If you and Teddy were to fill his shoes, you had to grow up. He waved his strict rod above my head -- and I obeyed. Between us two, I was glad to see you run after Teddy. You sneaked around and I pretended not to see you. But you were the child I adored, every time you did it. You were quite energetic and full of it. You almost had your brother beat in defiance!"

Anne knew she was treading on thin ice. "I wasn't as bad as Teddy, was I? Or did you know?"

"No, you were never that bad, my dear. You were my sweetheart. Oh yes, I knew, but I couldn't do anything about your brother." Her mother pulled Anne's head over onto her shoulder and combed through her hair. "No, my son was a bully, like -- my husband." She gave a firm nod of her head and reached over for her glass of wine to take a sip. "Does it surprise you to hear me talk like this?"

"No. I'm glad you want to talk. I want us to have mother-daughter talks more often."

"Your father thought that showed weakness, to small-talk with our children, for heaven's sake."

"Well, I knew they were bullies, but what you say surprises me. All the time, I didn't think you loved me. I thought you were avoiding me."

"I looked the other way to give you space, child. Annie, I have always loved you."

"If only I had known." Anne laughed and patted her mother's arm. "Oh, Mom, I've missed you."

Her mother grabbed her hand and squeezed it. "I've missed you too, for too many years. Want to start over?"

"I'd like that." Anne drew back and looked at her mother. "Are you happy, Mom?"

"Yes, I'm satisfied. Your father left all the financial and legal decisions to you and my trust when he graciously died. I'm content. Have I been a burden to you? I'm perfectly capable of relieving you of that responsibility. I think it's time you knew that." She chuckled, "You were so determined to carry on with the family business and sheltering me. I am so very proud of the woman you have grown up to be. What about you, dear Anne? Are you happy?"

She kissed her daughter's head for the first time in many years. "How about a glass of wine to celebrate our new found friendship?" Her lips creased a wide smile across her face. "I'm smiling all the way down to my toes." She wiggled her brightly colored toenails and reached for the wine bottle.

"Well, no thank you, Mom."

"Oh, not to worry. I only pretended to be a drunk to avoid your father. I really enjoy a glass of wine now and then." She reached for the carafe of red wine, but Anne stopped her.

"Not tonight Mother. Mama," she hesitated, "Mama, can I call you that again?"

Her mother nodded, "I'd love for you to."

Anne kicked off her pumps and wiggled her own painted toes. "You see, I'm off the stuff for, I'd say at least -- the next six months or so -- more if I'm nursing!"

"What?"

Anne then proceeded to tell her mother about the man she lived with on an island, when she lost her memory and found herself pregnant.

After Anne finished her story, her mother tossed her paperback on the floor. "My dear girl, that beats anything I've read in a long time. Now tell me you aren't going to at least contact him and tell him he's going to be a father."

"No, Mama. He never asked me to stay. He surely won't want to be bothered with a child."

Her mother made tsk-tsk noises and pulled her closer. "I think you're making a mistake, but who am I to tell my daughter about men?"

TWENTY-ONE

Eric missed her. Casey missed her. Her face haunted his paintings. He roamed the island each morning at first expecting to see her when he returned from his walk or later when she came down the steps. He interrupted his afternoons to go rowing. He watched the painted colt at the shore. Although he'd lived on the island for months and visited many times as a boy, now a Lise landmark identified every space on his home territory. *This is where she did this. Here is where she remembered that.*

He missed her chatter, her interruptions, her smell, and definitely, her body spooned into his own. He'd been such a fool to walk away the morning she left. His body ached to hold her, to make love to her again.

Pauli had helped him crate his paintings and carry them to the mainland. They both stayed and helped hang them at Josie's direction. Eric went to his home to shower and change clothes. Yes, he had a home on the mainland. It was one of those contemporary townhouses clustered around a courtyard. He'd bought two and had them built to his own specifications. Here he hid briefly until Lise invaded his dreams. He began to see her on the street and wait for her at the breakfast table.

One day there was a knock at his door. “Eric, darling, I haven’t seen you in weeks.” Josie slithered through the door. “Have you heard from that little sweetie of yours? *Hmm*? She couldn’t have a change of heart. I bet you had a fight that last day. Well, say something.”

“We did.”

“And you’re too weak a man to give her a call. Buck up, dear. Pick up the phone. All you’ve done is mope around this town as if you’ve lost your best friend. Admit you miss her.” The woman sat on his leather couch and crossed her legs seductively.

“You’ve known me too long. Despite your flaws, Josie, you’re probably right.” He waved a hand around. “I smell her in the air. I even brought her clothes with me when I came back to the mainland along with the dog. Sometimes I’ll open the drawer where I kept her things to inhale her scent.” He closed his eyes and imagined her by his side, picking up a shell or glass globe, holding it up to the sun like a child marveling at the color. “I hear her laughter in a restaurant and look for her. Even the dog misses her. He searches around the townhouse. Would you believe Casey sleeps on her shoes?”

“I’ve known you since before your wife died. I make it my business to know my artists’ habits. If it affects your art – it affects me.

“Well, the art show was a success. All the paintings sold, but one.”

"You kept the best one because it captured her smile and energy like none of the others." Shaking her head Josie continued, "You shouldn't have fallen so hard for her."

Those hazel green irises encircled with a ring of yellow haunted him. He worked in his studio from dawn to dark, stopping to eat when his stomach told him it was time. "I've packed for my teaching seminar and then unpacked. I can't decide about whether I need to go find Anne or maintain my schedule and travel plans. I can't call her. This isn't something I can talk about over the phone."

"You poor man, but I have news to make you happy." She waited for his head to lift before she continued. "I got a request for one of your paintings today. Some attorney's office in Charlotte wants to buy it for an unnamed collector. Now, who would that be?" Her head tilted at an angle.

If she had sliced out his heart with a dull steak knife, it couldn't have hurt more. "Why doesn't she call? She has my number."

"A woman wants a man to call her, you knucklehead."

"No, she's not like that."

Josie sighed. "Do you have any more paintings of her? We could send the painting shots over the internet." She pulled her digital camera from her bag. "Seeing as how they are requesting a special sale, we make more money, my boy."

"I have no more paintings at this time that I'm willing to part with." He leaned back on his couch and spoke quietly, shoving his hands in his pockets.

Josie stood up and quickly walked to his studio. "Now, I know differently. Well, would you look at this? Surprise!" She strolled between easels and oils, arms out and spun around slowly. "I see Lise, or should I say Anne, from every angle!"

It was true. There were sketches of her in charcoal, water washes and oils -- paintings of her on the beach, hanging sheets on the line, and one scene with the dog. There were fields of flowers and his whole island from different angles as seen through her eyes.

"I said I have no paintings I want to sell at this time, Josie. Drop it. Leave me alone."

"Well, don't get your big boy shorts in a knot. I saw this as an opportunity for us. If you are so wrapped up in love with this woman, why don't you do something about it?" She looked once more around her. "You are in love with her Erickson Armstrong. Go look in a mirror and see the look on your face."

She swished herself back to his front door. "Well, I have other artists to present to this attorney's client. If you aren't interested, I'll show him someone else. But if it's who we think it is, they won't be interested in another artist." She grabbed the door to pull it closed. "Eric, either get over her or do something about it. It's eating you more than that cancer did. You licked that. I'm afraid love is not something you can ignore. Call her." She pulled the door shut behind her.

Josie was right. Eric called for the dog and together they walked around Southport. It had been a while since he strolled the streets and enjoyed the town shops. Down by the waterfront, he sat on a bench and watched people, birds and boats go by. Summer was approaching and it had been over a month since she walked away from his island. Pauli drove by and waved. Grayson hailed him back. He parked the van by a waterfront restaurant, walked over and sat down by his brother.

"What you up to? I haven't seen you in weeks." Pauli stretched and placed his arms on the back of the bench.

Eric didn't say anything.

"I checked your house. It's all locked up. I moved the chickens over to join mine. That other house is good too."

"*Uhh.*" Eric leaned forward. He was afraid of seeing her again. He couldn't see her without wanting her and she didn't want a scarred man. "Would you deliver a painting for me? I'm supposed to go out of town for a while and I have something that needs handling now. I want you to take something to Lise, I mean Anne. Could you do that for me?"

"Well, sure. I can do that for you. Where I got to go?" Pauli leaned his head toward his brother, his mouth forming one wide grin.

"I want you to drive to Charlotte and take it to her at work. You've driven there before for Josie, haven't you?"

"I've delivered paintings to Raleigh, Greensboro and Charlotte, piece of cake little brother." Pauli patted his brother's shoulder.

Eric placed his elbows on his knees and began to form a plan. It was a brilliant plan from his way of thinking.

That night he took the painting of her hanging sheets on the line and placed it on his largest easel. Her head, her eyes and sun-tinted red hair appeared over the top of the clothesline. Below the flapping sheets, her jeans, bare feet with painted toenails half-buried in the sand. The wind blew the sheet against her body, draping her shape. Her hair fell across her forehead while freckles trailed across her nose. Salt air and sand, sea oats and laughing gulls garnished the six foot painting. Details only a beach lover could enjoy peppered the canvas. His gaze flowed up and around and down again in a continuous movement enjoying the motion and vibrancy of the work.

Pleased with the finished piece, he turned the painting over and took a two-inch brush from its stand. Grayson painted boldly, "Lise, I love you with my whole being. Come back to me. Forgive me. Love me. Marry me. Yours forever, Grayson" He painted the living words across the back of his canvas and later carefully packed the painting in a crate for Pauli to deliver. It was the first time in weeks he slept well.

***

"Make sure she gets it, Pauli. You deliver it personally to her. Don't leave it with her secretary. You wait to see her. Can you do that for me?" He helped his brother load the crate into the van. "I'm leaving today for the Nantucket school. But if she gives you an answer, you can reach me at these numbers." He shoved a folded list of his schedule into his brother's shirt pocket and waved him off on his journey.

"Deliver the painting to Annie and wait for her answer. Got it." Pauli slammed the door to his van.

Eric drove to a nearby airport and took his scheduled flight to Nantucket and later that week to Heathrow Airport.

***

Pauli had made long distance deliveries before for the gallery. His patience helped in the traffic and he enjoyed the change of scenery on these trips. Charlotte had its arenas, speedways and traffic, but he maneuvered his vehicle into a tall building's parking lot and slid the crate onto his dolly with little trouble. Someone held the door for him while he used the service elevator up to her office.

The quiet coolness of the hallway seduced Pauli into forgetting things. He approached the woman at the desk. Something about her reminded him of Josie.

He pulled the card from his back pocket and read, "I have a delivery for Anne Basnight from Erickson Armstrong." He gave her one of his special grins. The woman reached for her telephone and made a quick inquiry. Within seconds, Anne opened her door. Her face faded as if she was expecting someone else, but she welcomed Pauli into her office.

"Pauli, how good to see you. You're looking well. Is everything alright?"

Being in the Queen city excited Pauli with its crowds of people and noise. His mind went into overload. "Miss Lise, I mean Annie, Eric sent this to you. I drove it all the way. He said to be sure you saw it and see if you liked it." He carefully removed the painting, front side facing out, from the crate and stood aside while Anne's gaze prowled the canvas. "I like it a lot, don't you? He wants to make sure you like it before I leave." He held the painting by one corner as he searched her walls for a space.

It was her favorite painting. She pulled her blouse down over her slacks and flattened her hands over her stomach. She didn't think she was showing yet although she thought she felt the baby a couple of times in the past week. *Almost four months pregnant and the father has finally gotten around to acknowledging our brief affair. Well, damn! Wonders never cease.* "Did he say anything, Pauli? Is there a letter or message for me?"

He pulled a gallery pin hanger from his pocket and showed her his special hammer. He leaned the painting against the wall. "I'll hang it for you. Pauli is good at hanging pictures. I help in the gallery." He pointed over her credenza directly across from her desk. "That's a perfect place. What do you think?" He turned to see her nod.

He carefully removed his shoes and climbed up to measure the center. As he stabbed the hanger into the wall, she felt her heart pierce. He jumped down and lifted the huge canvas up. "Here, is this good?" He looked for her approval and gave her a big smile.

It was hard to believe that they were brothers. Their features were similar, but it was hard to see anything but the contrasting moodiness of Grayson compared to the focused face of Pauli. She nodded. "That's very good. Are you sure, there is no message? Did Grayson, I mean Eric, say anything for you to tell me?"

He shook his head, replacing his small hammer into a slot on his pants leg. "It's heavy enough to need two hangers. If this is good, I'll put up the other, ok?"

She swung her chair towards the window and wiped a tear away. Pauli turned the painting, backside facing outward and leaned it against the credenza as he worked on the second hanger. She heard him tapping on the wall and when he jumped down this time, she didn't turn to look until he asked once more for her approval. "There, that sure looks pretty. Sorta goes with the greens and blues of your office, doesn't it?"

"It's very nice, Pauli." She'd had the office redecorated since her return. Now an artist had sent her a gift to decorate the walls. Eric had sent her a painting to remind her of their shared time together. "That was very kind of him. You tell him I thank him for his gift. Can you do that for me?"

"I'll tell him. I'll tell him you liked the painting. Ok. Pauli is going now."

"Why didn't he come? Why didn'the bring the painting?"

"He had to be away. I did a good job, though delivering it, didn't I?"

"Yes. You did and I appreciate it. Wait. Let me write him a thank you note. Do you have a minute?"

"Sure. This is a big town. Real big. I never seen so many cars." He went to the window and looked out. Then, he straightened the paperweight on her desk, aligned the papers and folders as she wrote a brief emotionless note and tucked it into an envelope.

"See, this should go here." He re-aligned her pencil and pen set on her desk. "That looks better." Then Pauli waved and shut the door leaving her alone in her office.

Anne slid her chair back from the desk. She watched the door for a full ten minutes expecting Grayson to come barging in, but he never did. She patted her stomach and said, "Daddy sent us a gift. Isn't that nice? When you are a big girl, I'll tell you the story about that painting. It's about the spring I spent on the Outer Banks with your Daddy."

TWENTY-TWO

Eric squinted at the overseas long-distance number again while he waited to be connected. The trim secretary standing by the desk offered to help, but he shook his head. "Sorry, I'm having trouble reaching this number. I'll give you back your desk in just a moment." He dialed Pauli's number again and checked his watch knowing six hours separated the two brothers.

After the phone rang three times, Pauli answered. "Armstrong's Grocery, how can I help you?"

"Pauli, it's me, Eric. What did she say? You haven't called me. What did Annie say when you showed her the painting?" His words caught in his throat. Was that his blood pounding in his ears or a sound in the line?

"She said thank you. I have a note she wrote you. Want me to read it?"

"A note?" A note could only be a disappointing response to his proposal.

"Yes, open it. Read it to me."

Her message was brief with a humble thank you for his gracious gift. *Mercy! She doesn't answer my question.* "I'll be home in a few weeks. But if she calls, you'll get word to me?" He still hoped he would hear from her.

"Yep, I'll let you know. I have your schedule. Hey, Mr. Armstrong, send me a postcard and I'll stick it up on the board here at the store."

Pauli's smiling voice comforted him. "I'll do that, brother. You take care." Eric hung up worried. If he hadn't promised to come on this teaching trip, he could have delivered the painting himself. He thought the picture said it all. What didn't she understand? There had to be a mistake. He couldn't believe Lise - Anne sent no answer, merely a thank you note.

The secretary tapped her desk politely, waiting for him to leave so she could return to her late afternoon work. He pushed himself up and walked down the hall to the men's room where he splashed water on his face. Drying his hands, he resigned himself to waiting through the trip to get back home and sort out the mess. He couldn't call her now. He wanted to see her in person.

***

Two weeks later, a fellow painter stopped Eric in the hall. "This whole program with these special students has got to be one of the most rewarding experiences in my career. Thanks for asking me to join you."

"You're welcome. Downs Syndrome children and brain damaged students, whatever their ages are so willing to try new things. They love the experience." Grayson remembered Lise's eagerness to have a child and knew working with these children would lift her spirits. Lise again, not Annie, he remembered. She still pestered his mind for thought and attention.

"Well, we're halfway through the program. I'd like to do it again if I can work it out on my schedule." His longhaired companion clapped him on the shoulder. "What next? Boat or train to the next school? I can never remember the schedule."

"We leave this evening by train. You've made a difference. Thank you for coming." Eric knew the team's work touched the teachers' lives, as well as the students.

Together they walked back into the classroom. Eager students drew, painted, and sculpted mounds of clay. Their concentration over their work was remarkable. Eric reminisced, "This reminds me of when I was younger and a youth hostel traveler here in Europe, painting and drawing as I traveled across the continent."

An older woman came up to them, "Will you consider coming again next year? This is wonderful what you do." She was the mother who helped finance and plan the whole project. Her tired eyes reflected her hope that he'd return.

Eric thought it would be something to look forward to, especially if Lise, Anne, didn't want him. "I can't commit for next year yet. Next year is a long way off. For now I miss the solitude of my studio, my walks on the beach and…." He missed Lise. He couldn't wait to get back home.

TWENTY-THREE

"Miss Basnight, there's a Mr. Armstrong here to see you." Anne knew her prim assistant was used to stonewalling callers and listened on the intercom as Ilea-Jean said, "I'm sorry, perhaps she stepped --"

Of course, Grayson, her Eric would have nothing to do with waiting. Anne wasn't surprised to see him push open the door to her plush office. He paced across the width of the room and stood at the front of her desk. His knuckles pressed down on the smooth surface as he leaned over. "Why not?" His new eyebrows almost met over his nose. Alarmed but amused at seeing him with hair on his face and head, she smiled.

"I can't believe after months of hearing nothing that you are standing in my office." She pulled her new maternity jacket down and stayed glued to her chair.

"What do you have to say for yourself?" His hair curled in short waves around his ears and he'd tied a piece of something around a rat tail at his nape. She was afraid to answer, as if acknowledging him, would make his vision evaporate. She reached out to test her vision. Anne pulled a curl of gray hair on his forehead. It tugged back.

"Hey!" His gray eyes perfectly matched the silk shirt he'd stuffed into pressed jeans. He gained a bit of weight. An arty silver buckle clasped a tooled leather belt at his waist.

"Eric, it's good to see you. Are you in town for a show?" Anne was afraid to stand up and pulled her chair in tighter so he couldn't see her swollen stomach. A warm tingling started at her chest and spread downward. He had come to see her. Maybe he still cared for her.

"There's no show. I'm here because we have some unfinished business. Well? I want your answer, face to face."

"What do I have to answer about what?" Her fingers wanted to touch his face and run down his shoulders. Would he repel her stroking?

"What is your answer to my question, the one Pauli brought you. I've waited a month for a response and heard nothing. I can't believe you didn't write, call or come back." His hand brushed his hair self-consciously. "Don't you care about me?"

Anne answered with a husky voice. "I care very much." She was afraid of exposing herself. She'd dreamed of this moment every day since she left his island. "Of course I care, but what are you talking about. I waited to hear from you - that you wanted me, that you loved me…"

"Thank God."

His fragrance made her dizzy as she breathed in his smells. She'd never stopped using the soap he used on the island either.

He walked around her desk and pulled her up. His lips greedily covered hers. His hands held her face.

She had no time to resist as her arms crushed against his chest in the embrace. Afraid to lift them up to expose herself and her child to his body, she pulled back.

"What is it?" His impatient tone mocked her.

"I feel like the first day I saw you on the island. We kept asking each other questions." She folded her hands over her stomach and looked down. "There's been a -- a new development."

"What?" His gaze wouldn't leave her face. "I do love you. You must know that."

"Miss Basnight, is everything alright?" Ilea-Jean stood at the door. Obviously, she had been watching the past few minutes.

"Yes, everything's just fine. Please close the door as you leave." Anne smiled up to him. Her arms reached around his neck as she pressed her chin against his shoulder. "So much has happened since I saw you last. But what question are you talking about? I never got a letter from you, only the painting." She nodded to the large canvas on the wall above her credenza.

Eric stared at the beach scene he painted. The joy in Annie's expression displayed total trust and love. That's what he felt as he painted it.

"I love that painting. It brings me so much joy."

"You didn't have it framed?"

"Pauli hung it when he was here." Her lips formed an O.

"You never saw the back of the canvas."

"No. What do you mean? Pauli brought it in and hung it for me right there. Why would I look at the back? I thanked him. I wrote you a note. I thought it was a going away gift." Her gaze left the painting to find his eyes. She grabbed his hands. "I loved it. I'd rather have you, but the painting said so much to me I couldn't complain."

"It didn't say enough. Wait." He strode across the room to lift the large canvas down from and turned it around so she could read the back.

"Oh, no!" She giggled. "I never saw it. I swear. I never saw that." She began laughing as she walked over and let her fingers run across his words of love, his apology and his proposal. "You do love me."

He set the painting on the floor and dropped on one knee. "I do love you. I want you to marry me. I want us to have babies and live on the ocean. I want you." His gaze clung to her face as he pulled a ring box from his pocket.

"Ah well, you poor blind man. Let me draw your attention lower, if you please. Pulling his hand, she tugged him up and placed one palm on her stomach. "The babies are coming - sooner than you think." Did she feel a butterfly tumble against her stomach as his palm pressed on her belly?

Smiling, he said, "I felt that. Is he mine? Not some store bought seed?"

"Of course. He is a she, Daddy. Meet Ella Gray, your daughter. I've named our child for her grandmother and, well, a man I fell in love with one spring. Maybe we need to sit down." She indicated the pair of chairs by the coffee table and pulled a framed picture off her desk.

He babbled, "What? Why didn't you tell me?"

"Hush." She placed a finger against his lips.

"I'll move here so you can continue to work, if that's what you want. We'd miss the beach but I can paint anywhere if I have you close. I don't understand why you're still here. Good Lord, you lost your memory because of the pressure." His hands went out to the office surroundings. "I thought you wanted to escape, but I'll help you if you want all this."

"Oh, I do. I mean I do want to get away from all this, but I didn't know where to go after I came back." She smiled at him. "When I thought you didn't want me, I didn't think you'd want our child."

"What?"

She handed the framed picture to him. "Our child's name is Ella Gray. I hope she has your eyes and mouth."

"You have a wonderful mouth. If she has your mouth, I'll have to beat the boys away from the door." He kissed her again and then reached for the shadowy picture. He could barely discern the shapes of the sonogram. He ran his fingers over the feet with tiny toes and hands. "She'll have your hair." He smiled as he ran his fingers through his own short shag.

"It must have been that first time or one of your little soldiers found a way around another time. It doesn't matter. She'll be here in December." She kissed him again and walked back to her desk. "Excuse me; I need to do something, right now."

Picking up the phone, Lise asked him, "You do want us both, don't you? I still have my brother's house or we can add onto your grandparent's home. I'd sort'a like to live at Ted's, if that's all right with you."

"I'd camp on the mosquito-infested marsh as long as I'm with you and I can still paint. Your brother's house is fine. There are more rooms for all the children we're going to have." A salacious grin spread across his face.

"Good, I wanted to hear that." She spoke into the phone. "Richard, this is Anne Basnight. Fine, thank you. Are you still interested in purchasing my brokerage firm? It was in that package you gave me before I left on vacation a few months ago. Does the 90 day option still work for you? Yes, for your expansion." She opened the drawer and pulled out the thick tan envelope she'd carried to the shore on that eventful weekend.

She waited a few minutes listening to the other end of the conversation. "Yes, the terms we discussed are still satisfactory. Have your attorneys send the papers over to mine." She nodded. "Yes, next week would be fine." She wrote something in her calendar and smiled up at Eric.

For the second time that morning, his mouth was agape. "You're selling the family business? Not because of me, I hope."

"No, for us and Ella-Gray." She walked back to him and sat down. "I've been thinking about it for months now. I love my -- our daughter. I want to spend more time with her. Mother has enough money from Daddy's trust. With my trust and the proceeds from this sale, well, we'll do just fine." She grinned. "I shan't be your kept woman again and I want my own boat!"

"Agreed. Is there some place we can go?" He tugged at his open collar. "I'm already feeling claustrophobic here.

"My thoughts exactly. Follow me, my dear, wonderful man." She gathered up her purse, hesitated when she saw her attaché, but left it. "I know the perfect place to hang that painting in our new house. I want it hung so both sides show."

He put his arm around her shoulders and let her direct him through the pedestrian traffic once they were outside. He felt like he was walking on air.

"You didn't toss all my stuff did you?"

"I still have them." He kissed her again.

"I can't wait to get back into my Velcro sandals and did you keep that Hawaiian-print shirt for me?" She patted her stomach again. "I had to remove the pearl ring. Is that ok?"

"You forget you are marrying an artist. He'll paint you a new one." He placed his arm around her waist and walked beside her down the street.

ABOUT THE AUTHOR

Karen Dodd grew up on the coast, rarely venturing far from the shifting sands of the Atlantic Ocean. She met her true love at water's edge and they lived on a boat for several years. She and her husband sailed the eastern shores from Baltimore to Marathon before settling in New Bern. The award winning author continues to write about coastal towns and people.

Look for her River Walk Mystery Series that take place in historical New Bern, North Carolina.

****

www.ingramcontent.com/pod-product-compliance
Lightning Source LLC
LaVergne TN
LVHW091048080826
845145LV00002B/665

* 9 7 8 0 9 7 0 7 1 9 7 6 8 *